Amy Andrews is a multi-award-winning, *USA TODAY* bestselling Australian author who has written over fifty contemporary romances in both the traditional and digital markets. She loves good books, fab food, great wine and frequent travel—preferably all four together. To keep up with her latest releases, news, competitions and giveaways sign up for her newsletter—amyandrews.com.au/newsletter.html.

A CHRISTMAS MIRACLE

AMY ANDREWS

MILLS & BOON

First published in Great Britain 2017
by Mills & Boon, an imprint of HarperCollins*Publishers*
1 London Bridge Street, London, SE1 9GF

Large Print edition 2018

© 2017 Amy Andrews

ISBN: 978-0-263-07267-9

MIX
Paper from
responsible sources
FSC™ FSC® C007454

Printed and bound in Great Britain
by CPI Group (UK) Ltd, Croydon, CR0 4YY

For Sam Walmsley
from the London HMB office,
who wanted to see a tattooed, bearded
motorbike-riding doc. This one's for you!

CHAPTER ONE

TRINITY WALKER WAS having a bad day. In a life that had been punctuated by bad days, it was a drop in the ocean. Sadly, they were beginning to have an accumulative effect.

She was twenty-four years old but she suddenly felt ancient.

She'd just needed three more days. Come Monday her government payment would be in the bank and Oscar would be walking through the school gates for the first time.

She could finally get some order to their lives.

Regular child-free hours to dedicate to a job that would bring in regular money for things like rent instead of relying on government support and a variety of other dodgy alternatives.

Couch surfing, shonky hostels, single room rentals in share houses and the occasional night—like last night—sleeping rough in her ancient Mazda, was no life.

Not for her or her five-year-old.

Every now and then she'd get lucky and land a job with some form of accommodation attached. A room, sometimes a small flat or bedsit. It never usually lasted though. More often than not it was Oscar's health issues that ended the job and therefore their housing. Yesterday it had been Terrible Todd.

Her big, ugly, bearded, tattooed boss who drove a motorbike and reeked of cheap cologne and engine grease. Todd had announced that he did, after all, want her to pay for the accommodation.

Just not with money.

He'd felt they could come to an *arrangement*. She'd walked.

Bastard.

Bloody hell, why even bother with a permanently stressed-out, exhausted single mother who wasn't even that much to look at? She was five feet four, her long dark brown hair was so fine it hung limply down her back and she was somewhat on the thin side.

And not the sleek, glowing, deliberate thin of a catwalk model. The stringy, wrung-out thin of a woman who'd been stressed and struggling to make ends meet for the last five years. She'd *used* to be passably pretty back in her size twelve days, but even a fairy godmother would baulk at Trinity's current state.

Hell, it had been so long since she'd even thought of herself as a sexual being it always surprised her when someone else did.

Someone like Terrible Todd.

And here they were. With nowhere to go and no money to pay for anything much until Monday. Homeless again.

Homeless.

The word cast a sinister shadow as a cold hand crept around her heart. Fear over the welfare of her child, always present, threatened to overwhelm her.

Seriously, when was she going to ever catch a freaking break?

Maybe she could impose on Raylene again for the use of her couch tonight. Just one night. They could go after dinner and be gone by breakfast so Raylene, who was also doing it tough, wouldn't have to feed them.

'Look, Mummy! Look at all the ducklings. They're hungry.'

Trinity broke free from the sticky tendrils of anxiety. She was sitting on a park bench about two metres from Oscar, keeping an eye on him near the pond's edge, but had mentally tuned out.

'Yes, darling.' She smiled.

Her own belly growled in hunger as she also smiled at the old man standing next to her son at the pond's edge. He'd brought the bread with him about ten minutes ago and Oscar had followed him from the slippery dip like the freaking Pied Piper.

The elderly gentleman had said hello to her and had looked down and smiled at an eager Oscar as he'd asked the man politely if he could watch him feed the ducks.

'Watch me?' The old man's fuzzy eyebrows had drawn together before he'd given a hearty belly laugh. 'Goodness, young man, you can *help* me.'

Oscar had beamed and for a moment, Trinity had almost burst into tears. It was utterly ridiculous. She didn't cry. She was not a crier. Tears didn't put a roof over her kid's head or food in his belly. But she was feeling so damn low after her brush with Terrible Todd, such a simple act of human kindness had restored her faith in people.

She thought the elderly gentleman might be about eighty. There was a slight stoop to his shoulders and his clothes hung a little as if he might have lost some weight recently but Trinity could tell he once used to be a large man.

A giant next to Oscar that was for sure.

Her heart filled with love for her little guy. He was everything to her. Her stars and moon. Her reason to keep striving, to wake up every morning and eke out a survival when everything seemed so hopeless. A dear little boy who had changed her life.

Who had saved her from a life going nowhere.

It made her sick thinking about the number of times she'd nearly lost him. Born at twenty-six weeks, with tiny lungs and a major heart condition, he'd had an uphill battle. Six months in the NICU including two major heart operations. Another three months in the children's hospital until he was finally discharged *home* on sub-nasal oxygen. Then the next few years being knocked flat by every cold and flu bug going, in and out of ICU.

Trinity had been scared out of her wits for nearly five years.

Although he hadn't been sick for over six months. She hoped that it was a sign and not just flu season being over. That he was finally growing out of his chronic lung condition as the

specialists had predicted, that his lungs were finally growing big enough to cope.

She really hoped so. He'd frightened her out of
nine lives already.

A group of three teenage boys who should, no
doubt, have been in school, were climbing all
over the play equipment behind her. They were
far too big for it, laughing too loud, talking too
loud.

The bread all gone, Oscar ran back and started
chattering at her, his voice high and excited. The
old man walked by, nodding his head at her and
saying, 'See you later, alligator,' to Oscar who
laughed as if it were the funniest joke in the
world.

'In a while, crocodile,' he called out after the
man's disappearing back, hopping from foot to
foot.

Trinity smiled, pulling his skinny little body
hard against hers. His wispy white-blond hair
tickled her face as a lump rose in her throat. Just
three more days.

She could do this.

A shout interrupted the hug and they both
turned to investigate. The teenagers had bailed
up the old man. They were shoving him none too

gently from all directions and the old man was not taking it quietly.

'What are they doing, Mummy?' Oscar said, anxiety trembling through his voice. She'd heard that anxiety too often during his hospitalisations.

The man stumbled and almost fell and a surge of red-hot fury flashed through Trinity's veins. *How dare they?* This was a suburban park in a reasonably well-to-do neighbourhood—it was safe. That was why Trinity had chosen to pull the car up here last night. They were nothing but thugs.

'Stop it,' he said, his voice strong and angry. 'You have no right to do this!'

'We can do whatever we want, old man.'

Trinity's heart hammered as rage took hold. Yes, these guys and the Todds of the world always thought they could do whatever they wanted.

She looked around—there was no one else in the park. *She was it.* Her pulse skyrocketing, she set Oscar down on the bench beside her. 'Darling, I want you to stay here and don't move, do you hear me? Stay very still.'

His little fingers clutched her forearm. 'Like when they give me the drips, Mummy?'

Trinity hated that so much of her son's young

life had involved needles and doctors and hospitals and pain.

It fuelled her anger.

'Yes.' She kissed his forehead. 'Exactly like that. Mummy will be back in a minute.'

She rose then, covering the distance quickly. *'Oi!'* she yelled. 'Stop that right now.'

The three teens were clearly startled enough to obey as she stormed up to them. There was thunder in her veins and lightning in her eyes. She was furious but there was a clarity to her anger as skills from a distant time in her life surfaced again.

These guys had chosen the wrong person to mess with today.

The guys laughed when they realised from whom the demand had come. 'Oh, yeah?' the beefiest one sneered at her. 'What are you going to do if we don't?'

'I'm going to put you on your ass.'

The old man looked bewildered, his white hair mad-scientist-wild. 'It's okay, my dear,' he said, a gentleman to the core despite his confusion.

There was more hysterical laughter before it cut out and sneering guy locked gazes with her before giving another, very deliberate shove, right in the middle of his victim's chest.

'I say!' he objected, his voice quivering with outrage, causing more laughter from the moron gallery.

And an eruption inside Trinity's head.

The rage she'd been trying to keep in check exploded in a blinding flash. She grabbed the hand of the beefy guy just as he was about to push again and in one swift, practised, if a little rusty move he was on his back, his arm twisted painfully in her grasp, her foot jammed hard against his throat.

His friends' eyes widened as he gurgled on the ground, clutching at Trinity's foot with his spare hand. A second or two passed before either moved, then one of them puffed his chest out and lunged. Trinity was ready for him, landing a solid blow to his solar plexus with one efficient chop, dropping him to the ground.

She cocked an eyebrow at the third guy. 'You want some?' she demanded, her voice icy. 'Get out of here, now,' she snapped, giving an extra little twist to the guy's arm before removing her foot from his throat. She pulled her phone out of her pocket. 'I'm calling the cops.'

The three guys didn't wait around; they scarpered.

It was only then Trinity realised how fast her heart was beating. Automatically she turned back to Oscar, who was watching her with an owl-like expression, his big eyes huge and unblinking.

She rushed to him, her hands shaking as she scooped him up. 'Mummy, you were like a superhero,' he whispered, his voice reverent.

Trinity laughed. A kid who spent three quarters of his life in hospital had seen a lot of cartoons and the superhero ones were his favourite.

'C'mon,' she said, 'let's go and check on your friend.'

She turned around to find he'd walked away and was almost at the road near where she'd parked her car. He walked hesitantly though, looking around.

She put Oscar down and they half walked, half jogged to catch up. 'Excuse me,' Trinity called. He didn't answer. 'Excuse me, mister?'

The old man turned around, his face blank until he saw Oscar. 'Are you okay?'

'What?' he asked, ruffling Oscar's hair. 'Oh,

yes, thank you, dear. I just…' He looked around him as if he didn't know where he was. 'I'm not sure why I'm here. Do you know where I am?'

A spike of concern knitted Trinity's brows together. Had the incident with the teenage boys traumatised him? They hadn't physically hurt him but she couldn't blame him for being shook up.

'It's Monno Park,' she said, laying a gentle hand on his arm. 'You came to feed the ducks.'

The man stared at the pond for long moments. 'Oh. Did I?'

'Do you live around here?'

The man glanced at the park around him and the houses on the street opposite. 'I…think so,' he said, his big hairy eyebrows beetling together.

Trinity was really worried now. Maybe this wasn't a reaction to his confrontation with the thugs; maybe he wasn't of sound mind to begin with? Maybe he had dementia? Had he wandered or…*escaped* from somewhere?

'Is there someone I can ring for you?'

'Oh, yes.' His face brightened. 'My grandson, Reid Hamilton.'

'Okay.' She nodded encouragingly. 'Do you know his number?'

His expression blanked out again. 'He works at Allura. The veterans' hospital.' He stood taller. 'He's a doctor.'

'Right, then.' She smiled. Not even dementia, it seemed, diminished a grandparent's pride. She felt a momentary spike of envy at that. 'I'll look it up.'

Trinity wasn't at all confident as she rang the hospital and asked for Reid Hamilton. If the man had some kind of dementia, who knew if the information was correct? She might need to ring the police, after all.

The phone picked up and a male voice enquired who was calling, then informed her Dr Hamilton was with a patient. Trinity was relieved that she was on the right track. 'It's about his grandfather,' she said. 'I've found him wandering in a park. I'm sure he'll want to know.'

'One moment.'

Trinity smiled at the man, who was watching her intently, rubbing his creased forehead as if it would help clarify things for him.

'Hello? Who's this?'

Trinity blinked at the brisk voice. There was an authority to it she doubted few messed with. But she was over boorish men. 'Is this Reid?'

'Yes.' The impatience in his voice could have cut diamonds.

'My name's Trinity. I think I've found your grandfather wandering around in Monno Park. He seems a little...' she dropped her voice, not wanting to hurt the man's feelings '...confused.'

'Goddamn it,' the man cursed, low and growly. 'I'll be there in fifteen.' And the phone cut out in her ear.

The low rumble of a motorbike engine always put an itch up Trinity's spine and today was no different as, fifteen minutes later *exactly*, a big black bike pulled up at the kerb not far from where she, Oscar and Edward—he'd asked her to call him Eddie—were standing.

'Ah, here he is,' Eddie announced with palpable relief and obvious pleasure.

Trinity watched as the guy on the bike, dressed in top-to-toe black leather, dismounted with a long-legged ease that spoke of many hours in the seat. His helmet was a sleek black dome—gleaming and aerodynamic.

A little hand tugged at her pants and Trinity glanced down at her son, who was even more bug-eyed than he had been witnessing her drop two beefy teenagers to the ground.

'Mummy,' he whispered. 'It's the black Power Ranger.'

Trinity almost laughed—he did look very Power Ranger-esque in his boots, leathers, gloves and helmet. But then he took the gloves and helmet off, unzipped his jacket and completely destroyed that theory.

Reid Hamilton was more lumberjack than superhero. He certainly looked like no doctor she'd ever met and she'd met many. He had endless blue eyes, a wild mane of dirty-blond hair, pushed back off his forehead, and a full, thick beard that was neatly trimmed rather than long and scruffy. He was big and rangy like his grandfather and she could just make out tattoos on the backs of his hands.

'Hey, Pops,' he said, smiling at his grandfather as he strode towards them. When he drew level he enveloped Eddie in a big bear hug, holding him close for long moments before clapping him on the back a couple of times in a very manly demonstration of his affection.

He pulled back and flicked a glance at Trinity. 'Ma'am,' he said.

Trinity, who despised everything to do with beards, tats and bikes and hadn't had an orgasm in five years, almost came on the spot.

CHAPTER TWO

THE NAUSEATING SLICK of adrenaline that had been threatening Reid on his ride from the hospital dissipated instantly at the sight of his grandfather. Pops looked pleased to see him and there was strength in the old man's arms as he returned the hug. He seemed to be in good shape.

But clearly Reid was going to have to get someone in to care for him in the mornings while he worked now he was becoming more mobile after his fractured neck of femur. Or at least keep an eye on him. This was the third time he'd wandered. Reid had figured with the cricket on the television nothing short of a bomb would shift his grandfather from the living room.

Obviously he'd been wrong.

'Thank you so much for ringing,' he said to the woman who stood staring at him with a mix of unease and something akin to distaste on her face.

He was used to the look. A lot of people didn't

trust dudes who rode bikes and had tats. And, God knew, some of them had reason. It didn't usually bother him.

For some reason, with her, it did.

She was probably a foot shorter than his six-foot-four frame and holding on tight to a kid's hand. The boy was skinny with hair as white and feathery as Pops'. He craned his neck, staring up at Reid all goggle-eyed.

'No problem,' she said. Her voice was cool, her expression tight, but, even so, two full, sensuous lips drew his gaze. There was an intriguing set to her jaw. Something told him this chick had gumption. 'I'm just glad it all ended well. I was worried.'

'You were?'

She started as if she'd said too much but she recovered quickly. 'Yes.' It was prickly and defensive.

'Are you a Power Ranger, mister?'

He dragged his attention from the woman to the child. His voice was small but it rang clear, full of awe. Reid laughed.

'Nope, sorry, little dude. But they are my favourites.' He presented his fist to the kid, who bumped it enthusiastically with his own pale, puny one.

'Mummy fought off the men who were being mean to Eddie like a Power Ranger,' the kid said conversationally.

The words were like a punch to Reid's abdominals. He glanced sharply at the woman who until a minute ago had been a complete stranger.

'Shh, Oscar,' she dismissed, shaking her head at her son, her cheeks flushed.

Instincts that had kept him alert and alive in the Middle East on two tours of duty went into overdrive. His scalp pricked. 'What happened?'

'It was nothing,' she insisted, her gaze darting to the nearby car.

Reid glanced at his grandfather, who was smiling blankly. Clearly he'd forgotten the events already.

'There were three of them and they were all pushing Eddie and Mummy threw one on the ground—'

The kid let go of his mother's hand to demonstrate, making a *pshwoar* noise as he lunged with his legs, dropping an imaginary person in front of him.

'And then she karate-chopped another one.' The

kid sliced his hand through the air with a *hai ya*! 'Then she told them to leave and they ran away.'

Reid blinked at the revelations. He believed them. Not because the kid was so convincing but because the woman wasn't quite meeting his eye. 'Really?' he mused, lifting an eyebrow in her direction.

'They were just teenagers. Anyone would have done the same.'

Sadly, Reid knew that wasn't true. Over a decade in the military had taught him that most people did nothing. But not this woman. This woman had taken on *three* people—*guys*—in defence of his grandfather. He took a moment to look a little closer at his grandfather's guardian ninja.

She wasn't exactly big and strong. There were fine lines around her eyes and on her forehead and he thought she might be about thirty. She didn't look tough, especially not with a mouth that could have been perfectly at home on a catwalk model.

She looked…tired.

But he'd definitely picked up on an inner resilience. The kind that people in war zones displayed. And he knew enough about the world to know that war zones came in many guises.

What kind of war zone had made her so tough? Crappy childhood? Dangerous relationship? He slid his gaze to her left hand. No ring. Not even a white line or indentation where one might have been.

Not that lack of tan line meant anything necessarily.

But he had a feeling in his gut about her. Something told him her resilience had come from bitter experience. And Reid always went with his gut.

'Reid,' he said, reaching out his hand.

She eyed it warily before slipping her hand into his. 'Trinity.' She shook briefly—firm and sure—before quickly withdrawing.

'And you're Oscar, right?' Reid said, turning his attention to the kid.

Oscar nodded and held out his hand for a shake. Reid smiled but obliged, shaking the kid's hand. Also firm and sure considering he looked as if a puff of wind would blow him over.

He glanced at the woman. 'Well, *Trinity*, it seems I am in your debt.'

Her eyes, tawny brown with flecks of amber, widened as she drew Oscar closer. Most women he knew would have flirted with him over that but she looked as if she wanted to bolt.

'No, of course not,' she dismissed, her gaze darting towards the car again. 'It's fine.'

Reid frowned. 'Be that as it may, how about I take you guys out to lunch as a thank you?' He checked his watch. 'What d'you reckon, Pops? You hungry?'

'I could eat a bear,' he said. He made claws with his hands and gave a little roar for Oscar's benefit. Oscar giggled.

'No.' She shook her head. 'Really. I don't need to be thanked. C'mon, Oscar.' She reached for his hand again. 'Say goodbye to Eddie.'

'Oh, but I want to go with Eddie and eat a bear.'

The kid looked as if he could do with a bear-sized meal. So did she. 'Sorry, we really must be going. We have plenty to do today.'

Oscar's eyebrows practically hit his hairline; he was clearly surprised at the announcement of such a full day. Reid suspected that was because there wasn't one. But the kid didn't push, just sighed and shuffled over to Pops.

'See ya later, alligator,' he said, his voice chirpy despite the resigned slump to his shoulders.

Pops stuck out his hand and they shook. 'In a while, crocodile.'

She said a quick goodbye too, ignoring Reid as she bundled her son into his safety seat in the back of the car. It was possibly the oldest car Reid had seen in a long time—about thirty years if his guess was right. Back in the days when cars were heavy and solid and *not* made to crumple. The paint job was faded and peeling around the edges and there were several small dings in the panelling where rust had invaded like cancer.

He'd noticed it parked here yesterday afternoon as he and Pops had gone for some fish and chips at Bondi. It had still been here on their way back last night. And as he'd left this morning.

It was rare to see bomby old cars in this street. Reid doubted there was a car in the entire neighbourhood that was more than three years old. He glanced inside as Trinity buckled Oscar in. The car was bulging with black garbage bags. On the back seat, in the foot wells and along the back dash. It was a similar situation in the front, the passenger seat and foot well crammed with plastic bags.

It looked as if everything they owned was in the car.

His scalp prickled some more. He was starting to get a very bad feeling about Trinity's situation.

She backed out of the car and shut Oscar's door. 'Goodbye,' she said, the cheerfulness forced as she smiled at Pops and flashed him a quick glance of acknowledgement before sliding into the driver's seat and pulling the door closed. Her seat belt was on quicker than he could blink.

Reid almost laughed out loud. This was a first. Women didn't usually object to spending time in his company. Not even the tats turned them off. In fact, these days, that usually drew them like a magnet.

But this chick couldn't get away from him fast enough.

Before she had a chance to escape, he knocked on her window. She shot him an impatient look but rolled the window down. 'If there's ever anything I can do for you.' He handed over his card. 'Please don't hesitate.'

She took it to be polite but Reid had no doubt she'd toss it the first chance she got. He'd known her for fifteen minutes but he already knew that. She reminded him of some of the village women he'd met in Afghanistan. All he'd been able to see of them were their eyes but they'd told him plenty about their relief and resentment.

'Thank you,' she said and rolled the window up.

She jammed the key in and turned it. The engine didn't roar to life. In fact the only sound coming from the front of the car was a click. Her knuckles whitened around the steering wheel as she turned the key again. And again. And again.

Click. Click. Click.

She undid her belt and Reid took a step back as she opened the door. 'It does this sometimes,' she said, her face tight as she reached down and pulled a lever before exiting the car. 'It's a battery thing.'

It sounded like a starter motor to Reid. He'd tinkered with enough engines in his life—cars, motorbikes and military vehicles—to know the sound of a dead one. Although if the battery connection was dodgy then that was possible too.

She walked to the bonnet and slid her fingers under the lip, lifting the heavy metal lid. Her biceps tensed beneath the weight of it as she secured it in place. Reid joined her. The engine looked as old as the exterior. None of the clean, sleek functionality of a modern engine. Just a greasy, blackened chunk of metal with years of built-up grime and neglect.

His arm brushed hers as he peered into the mess. He didn't miss her sideways step as she tightened all the battery terminals.

'That should do it,' she announced as she un-latched the bonnet and clicked it shut, giving him a wide berth as she all but sprinted into the car.

Reid stood on the footpath next to his grand-father as she tried again.

Click.

Click. Click. Click.

'Sounds like the starter motor,' Pops said.

Reid smiled to himself. His grandfather was getting more and more forgetful but, a car enthu-siast from way back, those memories were still fresh and vivid. 'Yes.'

He strode over to the car. Trinity, gripping the wheel, appeared to be praying for it to work. He knocked on the window. It was a few seconds be-fore she acknowledged him with a straight-out glare. But she rolled the window down anyway.

'Sounds like the starter motor.'

She blew out her breath, staring at the bonnet through the windscreen. 'The starter motor.' The lines on her forehead furrowed a little deeper.

Reid crouched by the car door, searching for the right thing to say. A wild animal was always at its most dangerous when it was cornered. And that was how Trinity seemed at the moment—wild.

'I've got a mate who's a mechanic. He'll fix it pronto.'

She seemed to contemplate that for a few seconds. 'Do you know how much it would cost?'

Reid shrugged. 'A few hundred dollars.'

She looked away but not before he saw the quick flash of dismay in her gaze. Her knuckles went so white around the wheel he was worried they were going to burst through her skin. He knew in that moment Trinity was just barely keeping her shit together.

'I can pay for it.'

'No.' She shook her head vehemently.

Reid put his hands up in a placating manner. 'Just hear me out. I said that I owed you and I meant it. Let me do this for you. As a thank you. I can arrange it right away and give you a lift home.' He flicked a glance to Oscar sitting quietly in the back seat as if he was used to such breakdowns. 'What do you reckon, little dude?'

'We don't have a home.'

Reid blinked at the matter-of-fact revelation

as Trinity admonished her son with a quick, *'Oscar!'*

He glanced at the interior of the car, packed to the rafters with bulging black garbage bags. He'd suspected as much…

'Ignore him,' she said, her laughter so brittle he was surprised it didn't shatter into pieces around her. 'Kids say the damnedest things.' Her gaze was overly bright, the smile plastered to her face so big it looked painful.

Reid didn't know why fate had landed Trinity and her son in his lap today. But he was standing at a crossroads. He could take her assurances at face value and walk away. Or he could step in. As she'd done for Pops earlier.

Reid was a big believer in fate. His faith in any kind of God had been destroyed a long time ago but he'd seen too many incidences of people being in the right or wrong places at the right or wrong time to dismiss the mystical forces of predetermination. Trinity and Oscar had crossed his path for a reason and if he could help them in some way, he would.

Part of his job was advocating for homeless veterans—why wouldn't he afford these two the same courtesy?

'I'm going to call my mechanic friend. He's going to come and pick your car up. Then you and Oscar are going to come to my house where we can talk a bit more.'

'Oh, no, we're not,' she said, the plastered smile disappearing, a determined jut to her chin.

'Trinity…' He didn't know why she was looking a gift horse in the mouth. He supposed a woman in her situation was wary about who to trust. 'You can trust me. I live just down the road. In this street. The big white house that you can just see from here.' He pointed at it and she glanced in its direction. 'It's my grandfather's house, I live with him. Don't I, Pops?'

Eddie nodded. 'He's a good 'un. Looks after his old grandad, real fine.'

She glanced from Reid to Eddie and back to Reid. He changed tack. 'Look…to be honest, you'd be doing me a favour. I have to go back to work for two more hours and I won't be able to organise someone to be with Pops at such short notice. I know you've already gone above and beyond and I know I don't have any right to ask but if you and Oscar could hang with him until I get back it would be a load off my mind.'

She glanced at Eddie and her face softened a little, her chin lost its defiant jut. *Bingo.*

'He's completely independent,' Reid said, pressing his advantage, although the thought that the dementia might progress until that was no longer true churned in his gut. 'You don't need to do anything with him. He just loves company.' He flicked his gaze to Oscar, smiling at him. 'What you say, little dude? Want to come back to my house and hang out with Eddie for a bit? We have a cat.'

'Oh, yes.' Oscar clapped, bouncing in his chair. 'Mummy, can we, please? Please? *Pleeease?*'

She shot him a withering look. 'Are you *kidding* me?' she murmured, her incredulous gaze calling him out on his blatant manipulation.

Yeah…that had been a bit of a low move. Not quite like offering candy to a baby but not far off. 'Look. The car will probably be fixed by the time I get back from work and you can be on your way.'

Suddenly her shoulders slumped and he knew he'd won. It didn't give him much pleasure, manipulating a woman who probably had few choices in life anyway. But he really wanted to help her if he could and he needed a way in.

She turned her head to face Oscar. 'Of course, darling,' she said. Her voice was chirpy and Oscar beamed as if he'd just found a million bucks, but as she turned to face him her eyes shot daggers right through his heart.

If looks could kill, he'd be dead for sure.

CHAPTER THREE

'DO YOU LIKE CRICKET, young man?'

Oscar's eyes grew to the size of saucers at the massive wall-mounted television screen. It had obviously been on when Eddie had wandered away from the house.

Cartoons and cricket were Oscar's two favourite things in the world. Maybe because one of his earliest memories was the captain of the Australian cricket team visiting during one of his many hospitalisations. Oscar had wanted to play cricket ever since.

'I love cricket,' he said, voice full of reverence.

'Well, come on, then,' Eddie said, pointing to a big, comfy recliner chair. 'Climb up. There's still a couple of hours before they break for lunch.' He eased himself down very gently into a more formal, higher chair.

Back in the familiarity of his surroundings, Eddie seemed perfectly compos mentis. He was pointing to the screen and reciting some stats to Oscar, who was nodding in fascination as if Eddie were some kind of guru.

A big old marmalade cat wandered into the room, tail flicking from side to side. It jumped up on the chair beside Oscar before collapsing regally across his skinny legs.

'That's Ginger,' Eddie said.

Oscar patted the cat as if she were the most precious creature on earth. Ginger, obviously approving, purred like a motor. *God.* How was she ever going to prise Oscar away from this paradise? Cricket on a big-screen television and a marmalade cat?

She looked around her. It *was* paradise. She'd grown up with thin fibro walls and then thin air during her two years living rough on the streets. Reid's house was like a freaking palace by comparison.

She was glad he wasn't here. That he'd left for work as soon as he'd opened the door for them. She hadn't been able to breathe properly since she'd clapped eyes on him so it was nice to reoxygenate her brain.

To be able to think clearly.

The fact that her car was about to be towed and fixed, which would cost money she didn't have, was uppermost but the surroundings were distracting as well. What would it be like to have grown up in a nice house with grandparents who loved you as much as Eddie clearly loved Reid?

Reid didn't *look* as if he came from a well-to-do suburban background. If anything his badass biker/lumberjack look reminded her of a few guys she'd met while she was living rough.

But he was a doctor?

What the hell kind of doctor? She'd dealt with a lot of doctors these last five years—physicians, specialists, surgeons, intensive-care consultants—and by and large they were a conservative lot.

How had the medical establishment taken to Reid?

As much as Trinity was determined to stay put and not give into the urge to explore the house, the need to go to the toilet got the better of her after an hour and she followed Eddie's directions to the downstairs bathroom.

She passed a huge kitchen and a formal lounge room as well as a bedroom, which looked as if it might be Eddie's if the handrails she spied were any indication. The bathroom was at the end of the hallway and was bigger and whiter and cleaner than the room that Terrible Todd had demanded sex for.

Hell, if his room had been this big and clean she might just have considered it…

There was a huge shower complete with a rose as big as a dinner plate. It sure beat the crappy showers at the service station she and Oscar had used last night.

A hot wave of longing swept over her and Trinity grabbed the vanity as it threatened to overwhelm. This was too much. Just all too much. She should be grateful to have this opportunity to use these beautiful amenities and take a break from her life for a few hours but the pressure growing in her chest wouldn't allow it. Things like this didn't happen to her. She *never* caught a break.

And that panicked her more than anything.

She used the facilities and fled from the bathroom as quickly as her legs would carry her.

An hour later the cricket broke for lunch and Eddie said, 'Who fancies a sandwich?'

'Oh, I'll get them,' Trinity said, jumping to her feet. It was the least she could do. 'You and Oscar stay here and watch all the analysis.'

Eddie's kitchen was the kind she'd always fantasised about having. Large and open and airy, full of light from the massive bay window that jutted out from the sink. Pots of herbs sat on the ledge throwing a splash of green into the mix.

A massive central bench with a stone top dominated the space. It was beautifully smooth and Trinity ran the flat of her palm back and forth over it, hypnotised by its cool sensuality. A bowl of red apples decorated one end.

Underfoot, there were large white tiles, which carried through to the splash-back areas, where an occasional coloured tile broke up the uniformity. She could practically see her face in the sleek white overhead cupboards. Stainless-steel trim helped to break up the clinical feel.

All the appliances were stainless steel too and reeked of money and European innovation.

The fridge was a gleaming four-door with an ice and cold water dispenser on the outside and packed on the inside with an array of beautiful food. Trinity's mouth watered and her stomach growled.

For the third time today she wanted to cry.

This was what Oscar needed. What she couldn't give. A full fridge. Proper nutrition. She did the best she could with what she had and he'd always had a notoriously bird-like appetite, but maybe he'd be bigger and stronger if she could constantly tempt him with this kind of variety?

Trinity shut her eyes, squeezing back the tears. *She would not cry.* 'It's going to get better,' she whispered.

Once Oscar started school.

'Just hold on.'

She opened her eyes, tears now at bay, and grabbed things out of the fridge.

It was closer to three when Reid made it home and Trinity was as antsy as a cat on a hot tin roof. Oscar had already become firm friends with Eddie and Ginger and she was dreading dragging him away from it to spend another couple of nights in the car.

If it was fixed.

She was going to have to talk to Reid's friend about some kind of payment plan for the repair. She hoped like hell he was open to it because she needed Monday's payment to source some accommodation.

Trinity's pulse spiked as she heard the front door open. She'd dozed off in the recliner with her son but she'd obviously been subconsciously tuned into the sound of a key in a lock. Oscar barely looked up from the screen despite being jostled as she practically levitated out of the chair.

She was fuzzy-headed from her nap. *She never napped!* She didn't have the time for such luxuries. Her body, though, was eerily alert as she met him in the hall. On high alert, actually, as his black-leather-clad frame strode towards her and butterflies bloomed in her belly.

The man walked as if he owned the Earth. For a woman who'd spent most of her life trying *not* to be noticed, it was breathtaking. He was big and raw and...*primal* and she couldn't drag her eyes off him.

'Is it fixed?' she blurted as he stopped to dump his keys and backpack on the hallstand.

'And good afternoon to you too,' he said, a wry smile playing on his mouth.

God, even that was primal. Full with a sensual twist that hinted at long, hot, sweaty nights and tangled sheets.

He shrugged out of his jacket and hung it on a wall hook. 'Pops okay?'

Trinity's mouth went dry as her gaze took in his chest. Not because of the way his plain black

T-shirt stretched across his chest and shoulders or how snug it sat against a flat abdomen. *No.* Because of the intricate web of ink covering both arms.

Invisible fingers trailed across her belly and the pulse at her temple fibrillated wildly. It wasn't from fear, although God knew it should be. Or even from the kind of revulsion she'd felt when Terrible Todd had caged her in against the storeroom wall with his tat-covered arms.

It was from…fascination. Between the thick waves of his golden hair pushed back carelessly from his forehead to his beard to the tattoos she just knew didn't stop at his arms, she couldn't look away from him.

It had been a long time since she'd felt attracted to a man and even then it hadn't felt like this. Oscar's father had been her first and an ill-conceived choice at that. She'd loved him stupidly, blindly—all the way to the streets. But she'd *never* felt this kind of pull.

This was biology. Chemistry. She knew it in her gut. She knew it a lot lower too…

'He's fine. Still watching cricket with Oscar,' she said, forcing herself to focus on getting out of here, something even more vital now her attraction to Reid was a living, breathing beast. 'Is it ready?' she repeated.

'Not yet.' He brushed past her, heading for the kitchen. 'I'm starving, what about you?' He made a beeline for the fridge.

Trinity ignored the question as her brain grappled with his *not yet*. Where would they stay the night if they didn't have the car and just how long *would* it take to fix? There was no choice now, she was going to have to ring Raylene and see if she could have the couch for the night. Reid had offered to drive them home; maybe he'd drop them at Raylene's?

'What do you mean, not yet?'

He dragged the bread and some sandwich fillers out of the fridge and placed them on the bench. He glanced at her, his hands resting flat on the bench top. 'Gav has to source a starter motor for you from a wrecker's yard. Believe it or not parts that old are hard to find.'

He said it with a twinkle in his eye and dry humour in his voice but it rankled. She pulled her phone out of her back pocket of her three-quarter-length capris. It was a basic model—no fancy apps or data downloads for frivolous things like Facebook and Instagram—just a standard, cheap, pre-paid package but, like her car, something she couldn't do without.

Being contactable and able to make phone calls was essential for someone with a high-needs child. 'If you could give me his number, I'd like to make arrangements about the bill.'

His gaze held hers for long moments before he said, 'I've already covered it.'

Goose bumps pricked at Trinity's neck as her hackles rose. 'I said *no*.' She kept her voice low but even she was impressed with the degree of menace she managed to inject.

He shrugged. 'It's done. Now…' He turned back to the fridge. 'Would you like some wine? There's a nice bottle of Pinot Grigio in here.'

She blinked at his back. Was he freaking kidding?

'No,' she said, testily. 'I don't want a goddamn glass of wine.'

'You're right,' he said, completely undeterred. 'I much prefer beer.' He grabbed two bottles and set them down on the counter with a light *tink*. He twisted both the tops before she could stop him and sent one sailing in her direction with a deft push.

She wasn't much of a beer drinker—not at

three in the afternoon, that was for sure—but she caught it automatically.

Keeping her temper in check, she tried again. 'I don't want you paying my bills.' He opened his mouth to object but she waved him quiet. 'I know you feel like you have to thank me somehow but you really don't. *My* bills, *my* responsibility.'

He tipped his head back and took three long swallows of his beer. Her gaze was drawn to the demarcation line between where his beard ended and his throat began. The thick brown and blond bristles of his close-cropped beard hugged the underside of his jaw line before meeting the smooth, bare column of his throat.

Trinity watched it undulate as he swallowed and leaned heavily against the counter as things south of her belly button went a little weak. There was just something so damn masculine about a big, thirsty-looking man drinking beer.

'Look, Trinity,' he said as he wiped the back of his hand across his mouth. 'Let's cut to the chase.' He reached for the loaf of bread and pulled out four slices. 'I'm paying your bill because frankly I don't think you have two brass razoos to rub together and, if I'm not very much mistaken, you need that rusty old car asap because you're homeless.'

He said asap as one word, as she heard American soldiers say it on the television.

'So,' he continued, calmly applying butter, 'how about you—?'

'I am *not* homeless,' Trinity snapped.

He sighed and shook his head as he added sliced ham to the bread. 'I was in the military for fifteen years, Trinity, and I have a very sensitive bullshit detector which at the moment is flickering like crazy. How about you drop the act?'

It wasn't said with any kind of threat or malice but it *was* said with an authority that was plainly not used to being challenged. Her pulse accelerated and, like some errant rookie soldier who'd been caught out saying the wrong thing, she scrambled to qualify her statement. 'I'm just… between domiciles.'

'And how often are you…between domiciles?'

'Only *very* occasionally.'

She'd realised while he'd been gone that Reid being a doctor could mean trouble for her. That it was mandatory for him to report any suspicion of child abuse or neglect. If it hadn't been for Eddie and the car, she'd have picked Oscar up and run like the wind.

'A rare night,' she clarified. 'Here and there.'

He smothered the bread in pickles and mayonnaise and slapped the slices together. He ate half of it in two bites, regarding her the entire time. Trinity didn't like being scrutinised. She'd spent the last five years flying under the radar so Reid's astute gaze made her squirm. Because of the power he could wield over her if he wanted to but mostly because of what it did to her body.

She felt the heat of it *everywhere*. The echo of it in every beat of her heart. It made her nervous and breathless.

Good nervous. *Good* breathless.

Her muscles tensed as he held her to the spot with his eyes. The man had clearly missed his calling. He should have been a cop. If he kept it up she'd probably start admitting to a bunch of unsolved crimes.

Or possibly have an orgasm.

'You should come and live here.'

CHAPTER FOUR

TRINITY BLINKED. IT WAS all she was capable of. She couldn't move or think or talk. Had she had a stroke? Or slipped down the rabbit hole to an alternate reality?

Had he drugged her?

'Wh…what?'

Okay. Good. She *could* talk…or croak anyway.

'Look, it's really simple, Trinity.' He scoffed the rest of the sandwich and wiped the crumbs off his hands by brushing them down the front of his shirt. Her gaze followed helplessly as the shirt moved interestingly against hidden muscles.

'You're homeless and I have a home.'

'But…' She shook her head, trying to wrap her head around such an outlandish proposal. 'You don't even know me.'

'No, I don't. But I do know you came to the aid of an old man today when you could have easily not got involved. And that tells me a lot.'

'I told you I didn't want anything for that.' Stubborn bloody man.

'I know. Which also tells me a lot. Look—' He held up his hands as she opened her mouth to protest and Trinity closed it again. 'I don't know what your situation is exactly but I do understand homelessness. I work with a lot of veterans who are going through the same thing. I think you're doing it tough and I'd like to give you a roof over your head while you get back on your feet. There are eight bedrooms in this house. I couldn't live with myself knowing you're out there in your car when we have plenty of space here.'

Eight bedrooms? Trinity didn't think this could get any more fantasy-like. She was sure she was going to wake up any minute in her crappy Mazda with her back bitching at her. Things like this just did not happen to her. And she'd learned to be suspicious of good fortune.

If something seemed too good to be true, it usually *was* too good to be true.

'Isn't this Eddie's home? Should you just be inviting total strangers to come and live in it without talking to him about it first?'

'Pops will be cool with it, trust me. Just think

about it, Trinity. If you won't do it for yourself, you should do it for Oscar.'

A trickle of fear oozed down her spine. What did *that* mean? Was it a threat? Would he report her to child services if she left? Every muscle tensed as her instinct to run took over. How dared he spend five minutes in her world and lord it over her about her son.

Despite her anger, his words struck at the very heart of her. He was offering them something she couldn't. It rankled but could she afford her pride? Pride had walked her out of Todd's door but her options were even crappier now. At least she had a working car yesterday.

She'd spent the last of their money on brand-new school uniforms and books because she hadn't wanted Oscar to look like the poor kid on his first day—she'd been there and kids could be cruel. She hadn't bargained on being turfed out of their accommodation. Or on the car breaking down.

She eyed him as he took another mouthful of his beer. 'I'm not going to sleep with you.'

She said it as much for herself as for him.

He half choked as he struggled to swallow the

beer, coughing and spluttering before placing the bottle on the bench. *'What?'*

'The last guy who offered me a roof over my head felt that there should be some kind of *arrangement* attached.'

'I am *not* the last guy.' His voice was low and tight, his knuckles white around the beer bottle. 'I'm not that kind of guy at all. Frankly I find the idea of bribing a homeless, single mother into my bed completely *abhorrent*. I'm sorry that there are douchebags like that out there but *that is not me.*'

His quick, angry admonishment of the Todds of the world was just about the sexiest thing Trinity had ever heard and it did funny things to her pulse.

'There is absolutely *no* agenda here. It's a no-strings-attached deal.'

Trinity couldn't believe it was that easy. 'You must want *something* in return?'

He shrugged, the whiteness of his knuckles dissipating, the tension in his shoulders melting away. 'I can't deny having a presence in the house for Pops when I'm not here would be advantageous.'

Trinity frowned. 'So you want me to look out

for him. Or like…be his carer?' She needed to get a job while Oscar was at school; she wouldn't have time to babysit. 'I don't have any qualifications.'

'No, I don't mean anything like that,' he assured her. 'Although if you've raised a kid then you're probably more than qualified to deal with a slightly forgetful, sometimes naughty, definitely cheeky eighty-year-old.'

Trinity laughed then stopped, surprised by the sound in the midst of such a serious conversation. Surprised she could even laugh at all in her predicament. But Reid's description of Eddie was so damn apt.

'I know you're finding this all a little too good to be true and you're probably not used to relying on anyone but sometimes good things *do* happen to good people, Trinity. Maybe it's time you allowed somebody to help you. Aren't you tired of constantly worrying about how you're going to make ends meet?'

Trinity was *so damn tired*. The fact he knew that made her want to burst into tears. But damned if she was going there again. She hadn't survived this long by crying at every hurdle life had thrown her.

'Trust me.' He smiled, wiggling his eyebrows dramatically. 'I'm a doctor.'

His smile wove its way around her ovaries and squeezed. But he had put her dilemma front and centre again. He *was* a doctor. 'What if I say no?'

He gave a half-laugh. 'It's a free world. I'm not going to force you to live all safe and sound in this beautiful house, Trinity.' He smiled the kind of smile that told her she'd be nuts to turn this down.

But that wasn't what she was asking.

'And there won't be any…repercussions?'

'Repercussions?' He frowned.

She decided to put her worst fear out there. She didn't want to be looking over her shoulder all the time. Living life looking forward was hard enough. If he was going to dob her in, she'd appreciate a heads-up.

'You're a doctor,' she said, stripping her voice of any emotion that might betray how desperately worried she was. 'It's your mandatory duty to report incidences of child abuse and neglect to the relevant authorities.'

The light slowly dawned in his eyes. He shook his head slowly, his gaze seeking hers and holding it again. 'You don't need to worry about that. I see *no* evidence of abuse or neglect.'

Trinity blinked back a spurt of unexpected tears at his quiet conviction. For God's sake—what the hell was with wanting to cry every ten seconds around the man? 'I can't even give him a roof over his head,' she whispered.

'You can now.'

Yes. *Maybe.* Not her roof but a roof nonetheless. If she had the courage to take a risk.

'Say yes, Trinity. Stay here with me and Pops. For as long as you like. Get back on your feet.'

Her brain turned his proposition over and over. On the surface it was a dream come true. She could have a base. A permanent base she could depend on. A chance to forget about her troubles and worries and save some money. Actually make plans for the future. Get back on her feet as he'd said.

But then there was the attraction she felt for Reid. That could complicate the hell out of things. It could potentially screw everything up. If she let it.

If she *indulged* it.

Which was stupid and fanciful. Why would someone like Reid be remotely interested in her?

Oscar chose that moment to wander into the kitchen, carrying an uncomplaining Ginger, who almost dwarfed him, the top half of her body clutched to his chest, the bottom half dangling down.

'Mummy, Ginger purrs so loudly,' he said, beaming at her.

A huge lump lodged in Trinity's throat as Oscar sidled up to her. He leaned his skinny frame against her thigh and rubbed his face on top of Ginger's head.

'Okay,' she said quietly, glancing at Reid. Even just saying the word felt good. As if all the weight had magically disappeared from her shoulders. For now anyway. 'Just for a short while though.'

Christmas was a couple of months away— being in her own place by then seemed like a worthy goal.

He nodded. 'Stay as long as you need.'

If Reid thought he was going to see a different side to Trinity once she'd agreed to his offer, he was wrong. She might have said yes but it was probably the most reluctant yes on record and she was clearly still not comfortable with the deal.

At dinner she'd tried to talk to him about making a monetary contribution towards their food and board, which he'd dismissed outright, and then she'd tried to make a bargain with him about taking over the cooking from now on so she was at least doing something to contribute. But Reid had shooed her out of the kitchen.

After years of army rations he enjoyed eating home-made meals and found cooking therapeutic. He'd told her she could sit and watch with a glass of wine if she wanted but she'd declined politely, a pleasant smile fixed to her face.

Which had been pretty much par for the course today. She'd been polite and pleasant all day but there was a coolness to it, a reserve, that kept him at a distance.

As far as he was concerned anyway.

It melted away with Oscar. Hell, even with his grandfather she was more at ease. But with him, she was cool and polite.

Not that it surprised him. He didn't know how long Trinity had been doing it tough but long enough to have built a shell of wariness around her. And he knew that time was the only antidote. It was obviously going to take her a while to trust him. She needed time to get to know him.

To believe that he meant what he said. No funny business. No strings.

I'm not going to sleep with you.

It had been shocking to hear her say it. To realise that a part of her *actually* believed he had an ulterior motive for inviting her into his home. A sexual one. It'd made him so angry he'd wanted to smash the kitchen bench top in two.

He didn't know who the guy was that had put the hard word on her but it disgusted Reid. He felt insulted on behalf of his entire gender that there were douchebags like that out in the world harassing vulnerable women.

They gave men a bad name.

The thought that he'd take advantage of her situation was sickening. Sure, Trinity had fight and spunk, two attributes he found sexier than a great rack or an awesome booty. But he could see beyond her prickly, standoffish, tough-as-nails exterior to the frightened, vulnerable woman underneath and all he really wanted to do was protect her.

It was what he'd done most of his life and he couldn't switch that off because he no longer wore a set of khakis. There'd been so many women and children he hadn't been able to help, but he *could* protect Trinity and Oscar.

He went in search of her after dinner. She'd told him she was going to put Oscar to bed and he'd assumed she'd come back down and sit with him and Pops for a while—if only out of politeness. But it had been over an hour and she still hadn't showed.

He was worried she was hiding away and he needed her to know that she and Oscar had the entire run of the house. That she didn't have to sit up in her room like some frightened little mouse. That they had several televisions in the house plus a range of DVDs or she could use his computer.

He stopped at the room where he'd dumped Oscar's bag earlier this afternoon but it was empty. In fact it didn't look as if it had been touched. The door was open. There was no rumpled bedspread. No open cupboard doors. No discarded clothes or shoes.

Reid frowned as he moved to the next room along, which he'd given to Trinity because it had an en-suite. If he hadn't been very much mistaken, she'd blinked back tears when she saw it and it had made him happy to throw some luxury her way.

The door was shut. If a closed door wasn't a big old 'keep out' message nothing was. He hesitated for a moment, prevaricating about whether to knock. The last thing he wanted was to encroach on her privacy. And maybe she was asleep.

At eight o'clock at night...

The strip of light at the bottom of the door told him the light was at least on. So maybe she was lying awake staring at four walls worrying about things she didn't have to worry about.

Reid gave himself a mental shake. He was dithering. Reid Hamilton did not dither. He was a surgeon, for crying out loud.

Or used to be anyway.

He knocked gently. Low enough to be heard but hopefully not wake her if she was asleep. There was silence for a moment, then a quiet, 'Come in,' that sounded wary and tight even through the barrier of the door.

He opened it to find a sleeping Oscar tucked up in bed beside his mother, his fine white-blond hair and the pale wedge of his cheekbone a contrast to the crimson pillowcase. A mangy-looking stuffed rabbit tucked in with him.

A surge of pride filled his chest knowing that the kid would be sleeping safe from now on. 'Sorry,' he whispered.

'It's okay,' she said, her voice low, her hand sliding protectively onto her son's back. 'He sleeps like a rock.'

Reid envied the kid that. He slept lightly and dreamed too much.

Trinity was chewing on her bottom lip, regarding him with a solemn gaze. Her hair was wet, or rather it had been. It was half dry now with dozens of dark, fluffy, flyaway strands, which made her look about eighteen and not the thirty he'd originally pegged her as.

Just *how* old was she?

She was wearing some kind of sloppy V-necked T-shirt that dwarfed her shape and fell off her right shoulder. He noted absently there was a hole in her sleeve as his gaze was drawn to the exposed flesh. Her skin was pale, and the hollow between her collarbone and the slope where neck met shoulder was pronounced.

He loved that dip. Hell, he loved all the dips and hollows on a woman's body.

Suddenly it was gone as she yanked the sleeve up. Reid blinked at the action and the direction of his thoughts. *Bloody hell.* What was he thinking? He dragged his gaze back to her face but she wasn't looking at him; her eyes were planted firmly downwards on a book she'd obviously been reading.

Good one, man.

'I…just came to check everything's okay.'

'It is.' Cool and pleasant replaced by stiff and formal.

He glanced at Oscar again. 'You know, you guys don't have to share the same room. There's enough for one each.'

'I know. It's what we're used to. We don't mind.'

Reid nodded. He hoped she'd start to feel comfortable enough to open up to him about her past. To let the apron strings out a little on Oscar.

'Okay. Well… I also wanted you to know that you don't have to hide away up here. Pops and I usually watch some television together each night. We have three TVs and subscribe to a couple of streaming services so there's something for everyone. I also have a stack of DVDs if you'd prefer and you're more than welcome to use the computer if you want to go online for any reason.'

She'd slowly shrunk back into the bed head as he spoke, clearly overwhelmed. Reid rubbed his forehead. 'What I'm trying to say is that you have the run of the house. Help yourself to whatever you want, whenever you want. *Mi casa es su casa*. Okay?'

She nodded. 'Okay.'

But she didn't look convinced.

CHAPTER FIVE

'*MI CASA ES su casa.*'

Trinity turned the expression over and over in her head during the course of the weekend. She kept waiting for the other shoe to drop, for the camera crew to pop out from a cupboard and tell her she'd been punked.

Reid's offer had been outstandingly generous and she understood that he wanted her to feel comfortable in his house, but that was going to take a little while. Who knew the luxuries of a fridge full of food and a pillow top mattress would be so difficult to adjust to?

But the street kid in Trinity was never far away. That person had been baptised in the ill will people wrought, not their generosity. She desperately wanted to be able to take a breath and relax but she didn't want to get too used to going to sleep with a full belly and waking up without a sore back in case it all came crashing down.

Two months. That was all she needed. Reid

was making it possible for them to have a place of their own by Christmas.

But even if it only was for a few days it was worth it for how happy Oscar was. He hadn't stopped smiling since he'd walked into Reid's house and Trinity swore he actually had some colour back in his cheeks.

For however long it lasted, she was glad that Oscar could have this bright interlude in his otherwise grey existence. They were used to doing it tough and they would again if this bubble burst tomorrow but, for now, it was a little bit of magic she couldn't deny him.

Or herself.

Like her and Oscar and Eddie heading over the road to the pond the last two mornings to feed the ducks. The rest of the weekend filled up with the cricket. And, right now, it was a spot of soccer.

The afternoon shadows were growing long across the back yard as she sat on the porch swaying gently in Eddie's old white wrought-iron love seat, watching him kick a ball to Oscar.

It was surreal and she had to pinch herself.

The old man was good with Oscar. Infinitely patient and encouraging and Trinity had watched Oscar's confidence in himself grow in just three days. Oscar hadn't had any male role models and, in Eddie, she couldn't have picked a better one for her son.

A foot fall behind her raised the hairs on the back of her neck. Quickened her pulse.

Reid.

Living on the streets had heightened Trinity's senses to danger. But this was different. Her heart didn't beat faster from fear of being threatened or harmed, it was from…*awareness.*

A sexual one. A primal one. An acknowledgement deep in her cells of a *man.*

She hadn't seen a lot of him over the weekend and it'd lulled her into a false sense of security. He'd worked Saturday morning then spent a couple of hours watching cricket with his grandfather and Oscar before disappearing into the room with the computer that Eddie called *the office.*

This morning he'd done a bunch of yard work. With his shirt off. His tattoos did indeed extend further than his arms. In fact his entire back was inked from the wings that stretched across his shoulder blades to the barbed wire in the small of his back.

The real estate between the meaty slabs of his pecs and his collarbones was also decorated but the rest of his torso was ink free. Who needed ink when there were flat, bronzed abs on display? And a tantalising trail of hair arrowing south of his belly button?

Trinity had tried very hard *not* to look at that trail and where it went. She'd mostly succeeded.

After lunch he'd gone next door and done their yard work too, also sans shirt. What the elderly couple who had apparently been Eddie's neighbours for thirty years thought of Reid's big, bare-chested, tattoo-riddled frame she had no idea but, according to Eddie, Reid had been helping them out since he'd moved back in.

A frosty bottle appeared in front of her and she started even though her street-kid senses had tracked every millimetre of his progress towards her. 'Beer?'

Trinity shook her head as Reid—smelling freshly showered, and clad in a T-shirt and denim cut-offs—stepped around her and plonked himself down on the other end of the love seat. She tensed as it rocked and protested under his weight, the steady rhythm disrupted. It didn't feel right to be sitting so close to him. Sure, a whole other person could fit between them but she was excruciatingly aware of the type of chair they were sitting on.

'Come on,' he said, waggling it at her. 'You don't want me to drink alone, do you?'

She quirked an eyebrow. 'That hasn't stopped you the last couple of nights.'

Too late, Trinity realised what she'd said and clapped a hand across her mouth. How many beers he drank and who he drank them with was none of her business.

Reid threw back his head and laughed and her gaze was drawn to his neck again as fantasies about trailing kisses up it slammed into her.

Mortified—about what she'd said and her neck fixation—she took the beer, the seat falling back into a steady rhythm again as he rocked it back and forth with his feet.

'Oscar's excited about going to school tomorrow.'

'That's an understatement.' Trinity was grateful that schools took four intakes a year these days. Making Oscar wait to the start of next year would have been unbearable.

'It'll be good for him to make some friends his own age.'

Trinity stiffened. 'Yes.' She hoped Reid was

talking about the unlikely friendship playing out in front of them between Eddie and Oscar and not making other judgements. He might not have any friends his own age but he was remarkably well adjusted for a kid who'd spent half his life in hospital.

'He never went to any kind of childcare or kindy?'

Trinity's heart thudded inside her ribcage; she was aware of the intensity of his gaze on her profile. But she kept her eyes firmly on Eddie and Oscar. 'I couldn't afford it.'

Once she'd shelled out for accommodation and food and paid bills there had been precious little money left and Trinity had learned to be thrifty. Being able to have Oscar in childcare even a couple of days a week would have allowed her to work more consistently, earn more money but then she'd have lost most of her wage to childcare fees.

Thank God for the public school system.

'You don't meet too many Trinitys.'

She blinked, startled by the change of topic enough to glance his way. 'No.'

'Is there an interesting story behind it?'

Interesting? For some maybe. Trinity would

have preferred parents who'd prioritised stability over a creative name. She shrugged and took another sip of her beer. 'My parents had a bit of a thing for *The Matrix*.'

'Ah,' he said, nodding with understanding. He'd clearly seen the movie. 'Well, they chose well. You take after your namesake, putting three guys on the ground.'

Trinity looked away. 'It was only two.'

She suffered more of his scrutiny as his feet kept up the gentle rhythm of the love seat. Eddie was teaching her son how to catch a ball now—something a *father* should be doing—and she clapped and cheered when Oscar caught one on his third attempt.

Oscar smiled at her as if he'd just caught a sunbeam.

'How old are you?' he asked finally as the excitement from the catch died down.

Trinity glanced at him again. She supposed if she were a different woman with a different life she might have batted her eyelids and asked him to guess. But her flirting skills—such as they'd been—were long dead and Reid was not the man to go reviving them on.

'Twenty-four.'

'Really?'

She laughed then, a short, harsh noise. She couldn't help herself. 'Yes. I know I look older than that.'

'No.' He shook his head. 'You *act* older than that.'

Trinity almost rolled her eyes. She was dealing with stuff he wouldn't understand in his eight-bedroom-house world.

'So you were nineteen when you had Oscar?'

'Yes.' But she did not want to get into that with him so she changed the subject. To him. That was what men liked, didn't they? To talk about themselves?

'How old are you?'

She'd been trying to gauge his age since she met him. But it was hard to tell with bearded men—shave it off and it took away ten years. She'd put him at somewhere between thirty and forty.

He laughed. '*Way* older than you.'

Trinity breathed easier as he allowed himself to be sidetracked but also felt her interest being piqued. Maybe he was *over* forty? 'Fifty?' she asked innocently, cocking an eyebrow at him.

He laughed again, a big belly one. 'Very funny. I'm thirty-four.'

So he had ten years on her. Maybe not *way* older but enough for it to be an issue—for some. Not her because there wasn't a thing between them. *No, sirree.* Not even a hope of a thing no matter how sexually attracted she felt. Maybe the age gap would be sufficient to stem the neck fantasies…

'Wow. That *is* old,' she murmured.

He grinned, completely undeterred by her statement, and it took her breath away. Not just because the man appeared to be impervious to insults, but because his smile was flirty and, if she wasn't very much mistaken, her mouth was curving into a smile as well.

She didn't think her smile was flirty but—oh, dear—this was not good. She was *not* to flirt with Reid. Or let his flirtations go to her head. He was being *nice*, for crying out loud. This was how people who could afford decent houses and lived good lives interacted.

Annoyed, she turned her attention back to Oscar. She drank half her beer in three swallows as her brain scrambled to make sense of what had just happened. Maybe she'd gone that long without any kind of *affection* from a man that her body had decided to take over?

Thankfully he didn't say anything for a while and Trinity decided if she ignored him he might go inside or out to play with Oscar and Eddie.

No such luck.

'What are your plans tomorrow when Oscar's at school? You'll be a lady of leisure.'

She snorted. Trinity had a lot of big dreams in her head. She dreamed of a healthy kid and a stable job. A house to rent, enough money to pay bills and put food on the table and a more reliable car. In her biggest fantasy she could actually afford a deposit on a mortgage.

She never dared dream of a life of leisure.

'Get my car back hopefully.'

Oscar's new school was about a half-hour walk from Reid's. Hopefully it'd just be the trip *to* school tomorrow they'd have to walk. They were used to the activity but at this time of year they'd both be a puddle of sweat when they got there. She'd investigated the bus options in the area but it wasn't well serviced by public transport so having her wheels back was paramount.

'Gav's going to drop it back as soon as it's

done,' Reid confirmed. 'You can use Pops' car to drop Oscar to school if you like.'

This was the second time Reid had offered her the use of the BMW. Trinity had an excellent driving record but there was no way she'd feel comfortable driving some classic car whose tyres looked as if they cost more than her entire Mazda.

'It's okay, we don't mind walking.'

He looked as if he was going to push but didn't. 'What else have you got planned?'

'I have to look for a job.'

'What kind of job?'

'Bar work,' she said, turning her head to pierce him with a defensive look, lifting her chin. 'Or cleaning jobs.' She worked hard at whatever she did and she refused to be embarrassed by the menial nature of the jobs she'd taken to support her and her son.

She'd made a decision to get her act together when she'd found out she was pregnant with Oscar at sixteen weeks. She hadn't wanted to raise him on the streets with a permanently stoned father and she knew she'd never get ahead by relying on government help alone.

He nodded, unperturbed by the information. 'If you want to use the computer, it's all yours.'

'Thank you.'

Trinity was grateful for the offer. She usually went to the library to use their computers for job searching. Using Reid's meant she wasn't limited to a time slot or aware of the next person hovering in the background ready to leap in when her time was up.

Her name was down with several agencies but she rarely got work through them because she was considered unreliable. Employers had always been impressed with her diligence and work ethic but having to bring Oscar with her or leave in the middle of a shift or not be able to come in at short notice hadn't made for lengthy stays at any one place of employment.

'What did you want to be?' he asked. 'When you were a kid?'

Trinity gave a half-laugh. *A kid?* God. Had she ever been a kid? She'd always seemed to be the adult in her house. 'I wanted to be Barbie.'

He laughed too and it was deep and sonorous and settled in her marrow. 'I think that job is taken.'

She lifted the beer to her mouth and said, 'Story

of my life,' around the opening, her lips turned up in a smile.

'You had Barbie?'

'No.' She smiled at him. *Again.* She really needed to stop doing that.

'This girl I knew had a zillion though. Barbie seemed pretty damn happy with her lot.'

Barbie's life was all pink campervans, glamorous clothes and a steady guy. It had seemed like bliss compared to the wrecking ball of her home life.

'And later?'

It hadn't really mattered what she'd wanted to be later because, at seventeen, she'd finally walked out on a life of complete and utter dysfunction, swapping it for one even more uncertain and dangerous on the streets but where she'd actually felt loved.

For a while.

Having spent five years in hospitals though, Trinity had entertained the idea of one day being a nurse. She'd even looked into the part-time courses on offer. In a few years, once their lives were on track, maybe she could enrol. Work her way towards a job she knew she'd love and even greater financial stability.

'I've never really been that ambitious,' she dismissed, realising Reid was still waiting for an answer. Her smile was forced now, definitely not flirty. 'Did you always want to be a doctor?'

Subject. Changed.

'Oh, no,' he said with a wide, self-deprecating grin. 'I wanted to be a baddie. Like the ones in the movies.'

The admission surprised a laugh out of Trinity. 'Not the good guy?'

He shook his head. 'The bad guys had cooler gadgets and blew up more stuff.'

Well, he'd succeeded. He looked pretty damn badass to her, with his arm tats taunting her peripheral vision and memories of his other ink taunting her inward eye. He owned the whole bad-boy thing. Tats, beard, bike. The type of guy mothers warned their daughters about.

Well, some mothers. Hers would have probably been all over him.

But she'd seen enough of Dr Reid Hamilton these last few days to know that was just a fashion statement. He'd taken in a single mother with a child—complete strangers—and offered them a chance to get ahead with no strings attached.

He was a carer for his grandfather. He mowed his neighbour's lawn, for crying out loud.

There was nothing baddie about him. He was the goodie. The good guy.

Dr Good Guy.

CHAPTER SIX

'IS THAT WHAT the tats are about?' Trinity asked.

He glanced down, rubbed his left palm over the tats of his right forearm. 'Nah. I got these in the army. It started off as a drunken dare on my first tour to the Middle East then one became two and then I pretty much became obsessed with ink.'

The army? So he'd been a doctor in the military? He'd been to the Middle East. She was bursting with questions over that but where she came from people didn't pry.

'And the long hair? The beard?'

He shoved his hand through his hair, pushing it back off his forehead before stroking his beard. He extended his neck and ran the backs of his fingers up the ridge of his trachea.

'I got out of the military at the beginning of the year. I was sick of buzz cuts and shaving and I needed a sabbatical. When I came home I bought a motorbike and I took off on a trip to ride all the way around Australia. I just…checked out.

Which wasn't conducive to shaving or having my hair cut every other week, which suits me just fine.'

Trinity could only imagine how wonderful it would be to have the luxury of *taking off.* Just *checking out* for a while.

'I got a call in August about Pops' fall and came home to take care of him but the beard...' He stroked it again, a slight smile curving his mouth. 'I decided to keep it.'

His whiskers made a delightfully scratchy sound Trinity felt deep, *deep* inside her. Reid must really love his grandfather to drop everything and come home to care for him. 'How far did you get?' she asked.

''Bout halfway.'

'Oh, that's a shame.'

He shrugged dismissively. 'Pops was more important. He's always been there for me. He took me in when my life started to go off the rails a little in my teenage years. It's the least I could do. I owe him.'

Reid's life had gone off the rails? Curiouser and curiouser. But none of her business. She didn't like it when people snooped into hers so she sure as hell wasn't going to snoop into his. 'He's lucky to have you,' she murmured.

So was she. And Oscar.

'Nah. I'm the lucky one. But one day, after he's gone, I'll be back out on that road as fast as my legs and a two-hundred-horsepower engine can take me.'

For some reason the news surprised her. She'd made assumptions about him being settled in suburbia based on where he lived and what he did even though he looked the exact opposite of suburban guy. She should have known the second he'd swung off his motorbike and taken off his gloves and helmet that he was a rolling stone.

'You don't like Sydney?'

'I *love* Sydney. It was where I was born and raised. It's my home. But I've spent fifteen years of my life with no control over where I went and what I did every day. And that was fine. I was in service to my country. I'm proud of that. But I'm also *done*.'

He tipped his head back and guzzled the rest of his beer.

'I want to go where I want to go and do what I want to do. I want the open road and freedom. I don't want to be tied down to any one place or one way of life any more. I want to stop where I want to stop and leave when I want to leave.'

Trinity didn't know anything about his life or where it had taken him but she'd kill to have what he had right here in suburban Sydney. She supposed that was the difference between *choosing* a transitory life and having one *thrust* upon you.

'I would have thought you'd have cherished the…stability of settling in one place after moving around so much. Of actually…coming home.'

Stability was *everything* to Trinity. She'd lacked it her entire life and she craved it as Oscar's father had craved the pot he'd smoked far too much.

His gaze met and locked with hers as he shook his head slowly. 'I think I was born with a wandering soul.'

Trinity believed him. She could almost see the lone rider in his wild-blue-yonder eyes. 'Well,' she said, turning her attention back to the catching lesson, 'to each their own.'

They watched the game for a few minutes to the steady rock of the chair. 'Listen,' Reid said, twisting his body in a half-turn to face her. 'I wanted to talk to you about something.'

Trinity didn't like the suddenly serious tone of his voice one iota and she stiffened as the possibilities flipped like a Rolodex through her head. Here it came. Her pulse pounded in ominous warning. She knew it was too good to be true. He'd given her a couple of days to get settled and now he was going to pull the rug out from underneath her.

It wasn't as if she hadn't expected something like this but she'd started to let her guard down, actually believe in her good luck. In him.

She was going to be pretty damn angry with him—and herself—if it all went pear-shaped. With Terrible Todd she'd politely told him to remove his hand from her pants and get out of the way or he'd have a sexual harassment suit jammed up his ass quicker than he could blink.

She wasn't sure she could be so polite with Reid.

'Okay…' She gulped down the rest of her beer and forced herself to look at him. If he was going to kick her out or put the hard word on her then he was going to have to look her in the eye.

'I don't want you to take this the wrong way.'

Oh, dear God. 'Just say it.'

'I'd like to offer you a job.'

Trinity blanked out. Her pulse tripped madly

as she tried to reconcile the calamity going on inside her head with his words.

I'd like to offer you a job.

Not, *I'd like to come to an arrangement.*

'What?' she asked, slowly letting out the breath that was screaming in her lungs for release.

'I think Pops needs someone with him when I'm not home. You need a job. It's win-win.'

She opened her mouth to protest. Even though she wasn't sure anything would actually come out. He waved it away. 'Just until you find something else and I can arrange something more permanent.'

He shifted in the chair so he was facing her more fully, his expression earnest as the swinging motion went a little haywire. He bent his right leg up, his foot resting on top of his left knee. The frayed edge of his denim cut-offs sat mid-thigh. No tattoos that far south, just golden brown hair, as wild and thick as the hair on his head.

His feet were bare. And *big*.

She pushed back highly inappropriate thoughts about the correlation between foot size and the size of what a guy was packing between his legs.

What was the matter with her? The man had been scrupulously above board with her—hadn't once checked out her legs or ogled her boobs as Terrible Todd had done—and she was thinking about the size of his package.

She scrambled for something useful to say. 'Do you mind me asking…is it Alzheimer's?' She'd been wondering, had assumed it *was*, or something like it, but now she was grateful just to be able to say something—anything—as her brain grappled with his job offer.

And the size of his feet.

'Yes. It was diagnosed when he fractured his hip a couple of months ago.'

'I'm sorry,' Trinity murmured, glancing at Eddie laughing and playing with Oscar. He might not be young but there was still a vitality to the old man.

'It's early stages and he's on a drug trial which has had very promising results so they're hoping we'll halt or at least slow the progress.'

Trinity nodded, turning her thoughts to the next thing. 'He broke his hip?'

'Yes. His neck of femur, actually. It's pretty common in someone his age but it's been pinned. He had some complications with a wound infection, which delayed his recovery, but he's only on twice-weekly physio now and he gets around quite well without an aid as you can see.'

'Is that why he has the higher chair?'

'Yes. While he's in the recovery phase. The therapists at my work do his physio so I normally either take him with me or come back for him. It would be very convenient for me to have someone who can drive him to his appointment and back home again as he hasn't been cleared to drive again yet and, frankly, I'm not sure he should still have his licence but I'll worry about that when we get to it.'

In that moment Trinity felt an affinity with Reid. Caring for an aging grandfather involved the same forward planning as caring for a child and she admired the hell out of him for it. Had there been other family who hadn't stepped up or had Reid volunteered?

'Well?' he asked. 'What do you reckon? I leave here at eight Monday to Saturday and I'm home by two. You'll be able to drop Oscar to school each morning and I'll be home for when you need to pick him up.'

Trinity wasn't sure about this at all. If she was spending all the school hours with Eddie, she wasn't out there actually finding a job that could sustain her after she and Oscar left. But, there was no denying, she felt an obligation towards Reid and Eddie.

'I'll probably be out for about half an hour in the mornings, maybe longer some days, dropping Oscar at school and getting him settled there. What if Eddie...?'

She didn't finish the sentence because the list of things that could happen to an eighty-year-old man suffering from early-stage dementia and prone to broken bones seemed too long to contemplate.

'Pops doesn't need someone with him every minute of the day. He doesn't need a carer or a jailer either. I'll just rest easier knowing someone is around looking out for him. You'd be more like a...companion.'

A companion. It sounded very Victorian.

'You don't have to stay home with him looking at four walls or watching the telly all day either, if you don't want to. Get out of the house with him. Pops loves to go driving. He loves a beach, a museum, a train ride into the city. And he's great company.'

It didn't sound like a hardship. She liked Eddie and Oscar adored him but still Trinity hesitated.

She'd learned a long time ago not to rely on any-one and some habits were hard to break. 'Don't they have agencies for this kind of thing?'

'Yes, they do. And I will absolutely set about organising something more permanent. But I think it's going to take a little time because I'll probably also advertise privately. I want to make sure that whoever I employ is compatible with Pops. I don't want to lumber him with someone he can't stand or just anyone an agency might send around.'

Trinity felt a certain pride that he didn't con-sider her just anyone.

'The going rate for a carer is twenty dollars an hour. Six hours a day, six days a week is seven hundred and twenty dollars a week. Cash, of course.'

The colour drained from Trinity's face and she was grateful she was sitting down. *Say what now?* She'd never earned that much in a week be-cause she hadn't been able to work those kinds of hours. 'But I wouldn't be a carer,' she said, her voice faint to her own ears. 'I'd be a companion.'

'It's a comparable job.' He shrugged, once again waving away her concerns. 'I can afford it and Pops is worth it. Plus,' he said with a look on his face that announced he was about to lay down his trump card, 'it'll also give you another skill set. Some experience at another job other than bar work or cleaning that'd fit in better with Oscar's hours. I'd give you a reference too, of course.'

Trinity's brain buzzed. With that kind of money in two months they could not only be in their own place by Christmas but she could even have a bit of a nest egg built up. Or a buffer anyway. In case something happened—like Oscar ended up back in hospital.

She knew a lot of people would jump at the deal but, there was no way she could take that kind of money from him. Not when he was already doing so much. But maybe he was open to negotiation?

'Trinity?'

She shook her head. 'I can't take that kind of money.'

'You'll have earned it fair and square.'

'No. Those rates don't take into account the fact that Oscar and I are living in your house. Live-in help always get paid less.' She knew that from the times she'd managed to score accommodation with a job.

'That's totally separate to this.'

'No, it isn't.' Not as far as she was concerned.

'If you're going to pay me that much then I insist that you take out money for food and board.'

He sighed and shook his head. 'Trinity.'

He sounded frustrated and a little impatient but she wasn't going to be swayed. Even a couple of hundred dollars extra on top of being able to save her government support would make a huge difference. Enough to pay a bond on an apartment and have the first couple months' rent saved.

'I think two hundred dollars seems fair.'

He snorted. 'Two hundred dollars is slave labour.'

'If I had to pay rent and food out of that seven hundred dollars I'd have *nothing* left over and you know it. Two hundred dollars is more than adequate. Hell, it's a damn good deal.'

He stroked his beard as he regarded her through narrowed eyes. The rasp of his whiskers was utterly sexual. It was completely inappropriate for Trinity to wonder how they'd feel against her nipples. Or the inside of her thighs.

But she did.

In fact her whole body buzzed traitorously with sensations from an *imagined* action. A fantasy. The man was clearly not interested. He was looking at her long and hard and her nipples were two stiffened peaks brazenly trumpeting her arousal and he hadn't dropped his gaze once to check them out even though he *had* to be able to see them.

Hell, they could probably be seen from the moon.

This was highly inappropriate. The man had taken her in and given her *and her son* a place of safety out of kindness and a sense of obligation to her for helping Eddie out at the park.

And, if she took up his offer—she'd be crazy if she didn't—he was about to be her boss.

For God's sake, he probably had a girlfriend. Or a lover. Or a regular booty call. Or however the hell guys with bikes and tats described their relationships with women. Her nipples had no business flirting with him.

She folded her arms.

'Five hundred,' he said, finally.

Trinity swallowed. 'Three hundred.' God, three hundred would be a godsend.

'Four.'

Four hundred dollars? *Cash.* Trinity's head spun. That on top of her government support would be beyond her wildest dreams. Four hundred dollars *every* week.

Maybe her stars really were changing. Maybe she could finally take a breath?

'Done,' she said, straining her vocal cords to keep her voice strong and matter-of-fact.

He held out his hand. Trinity hesitated for a moment before she took it, her nipples still two pebbles inside her bra.

Maybe not touching him at all was a good policy.

'You drive a hard bargain,' he said with a smile as they slowly shook.

Trinity faked a smile and tried not to think about things that were hard.

On her. And the things that could *get* hard, on him.

CHAPTER SEVEN

REID WATCHED CHASE FROST flirt with Trinity through the window of his office that looked out over the large, open therapy room. He'd been flirting with her since she'd arrived with Pops almost an hour ago instead of working out on the weight machines to build up the strength in his thigh. There was a lot of gym equipment they used in therapy specifically to strengthen and tone muscles.

She was sitting on the chairs that lined the wall nearest the door and Chase was sprawled in the chair next to her, his prosthesis on full display. Reid gave a mental eye roll. The above-knee amputee never let the minor matter of a missing leg dent his game with the ladies. If anything he played on it.

Not that Reid blamed him. Hell, he kind of admired him for it. The conflicts in Iraq and Afghanistan had maimed many a good soldier both physically and mentally. Chase, however, aside from the distress of the acute phase, had been philosophical about his injury despite the numerous socket issues he'd had with his prosthesis and problems with phantom limb pains. Reid could hardly judge him for using whatever he could to his advantage.

The man had lost his leg to an IED—he'd paid a high price for his service and if that was what some chicks dug, then more power to him.

He just wished that, today, it hadn't been Trinity in his sights.

She'd been wary at first, keeping that polite distance she kept around him, but she'd relaxed quickly and was actually laughing now.

'The surgeon did a good job, Doc.'

Reid dragged his attention back to Brett, the latest casualty to have returned from the conflict in the Middle East. He'd lost his foot from just above the ankle and, now he was in the recovery phase, had been sent to Allura for outpatient prosthetics and rehab.

'A damn good job,' Reid agreed as he inspected the stump, 'considering how mangled it was.' He'd seen the pictures.

Reid knew, because he'd spent eight years of his life as a combat surgeon, the importance of what was left when the decision was made to amputate. There was nothing that could be done for the lost limb but forming a good stump was paramount for prosthetics and some surgeons were better than others.

He'd been one of the best.

But it also depended on the circumstances and where the patient was. Not all amputations happened in a fully prepped surgical tent. Some happened in the field through necessity and that was guaranteed to have a poorer outcome. Not just for life but for limb as well.

'I don't remember, Doc. Don't remember any of it. I think I was in so much shock I didn't feel the pain.'

'Well, thank God for that,' Reid mused. 'Because getting blown up usually hurts like hell.'

'So Chase tells me.' Brett grinned, remarkably chipper for a young guy who'd suffered a significant injury that would have far-reaching consequences.

He was already talking about competing in the Invictus Games for disabled veterans but Reid suspected it hadn't fully hit him yet. A bit like the pain from his injury. The road to recovery wasn't easy for anyone and Brett was probably going to find that the pain would come back to bite him on the ass when he least suspected it.

Still, that was why Reid was here. Not just for the physical needs of his patients but for the emotional ones as well. Getting on top of any depression, referring on to the right people was essential. Allura was a small, private veterans' hospital but it provided a full service and Reid believed in taking care of military personnel's mental health as well as their stumps and other rehab needs.

It was different from what Reid had spent the previous eight years of his life doing. It was more GP than combat surgeon. In fact, gloves deep in someone's gut, torn apart from shrapnel, or sawing off someone's leg, he'd never seen himself in the rehab sector.

Not in a million years.

But, with his plans to travel around Australia abruptly halted, he'd needed to do something while stuck in suburbia and he hadn't wanted to go back into surgery. Then he'd spotted this job advertised and, even though he wasn't specifically qualified for it, the hospital had been trying to fill the position for months.

They probably would have taken a trained monkey as long as it had a medical degree.

In a lot of ways he was overqualified but, when it was all boiled down, he was actually *perfect* for the job. An ex-military combat surgeon with an exceptional understanding of the injuries that he saw every day. And not just of the mechanics of blast injuries but the mindset of someone who had been in the thick of active combat; all made him *uniquely qualified.*

And it was a good fit for this stage of his life.

'Okay. Head out to Kathy. She'll start the preliminary measurements for your prosthetic.'

Reid followed Brett out, lounging in his doorway, shoulder propped against the frame, ostensibly watching Mario, Allura's head physio, with his grandfather. Mario was leading Pops through his therapy and Reid could tell that his grandfather was getting stronger with each session.

But Trinity laughed *again* at something Chase was saying and Reid's gaze strayed. He hadn't heard her laugh that much in five whole days. And it bugged him. It was none of his damn business but it still bugged him.

Chase had consistently crashed and burned with Kathy and every other female on staff at the rehab clinic. Not because he wasn't charming and good-looking, but because he was a patient *and* a player. One of those guys who had a *fluid* definition of fidelity. So, Trinity was new territory for him.

And, with her smiling at him and actually looking her twenty-four years for a change, he was flirting up a storm.

Smug bastard.

Did she think that because Chase had one leg, he was harmless? He hoped not. According to Chase, he'd got laid more times with one leg than he ever had with two.

Reid probably should warn her about Chase but he knew she could take care of herself. Maybe he should warn Chase about Trinity...

Reid would have given anything to have seen her moves in the park last week. Oscar was still talking about it despite her trying to shush him.

'Okay, Eddie, you're done,' Mario announced, reaching down a hand to help Pops up from the weight machine he'd been working on.

Reid ambled over, walking around the parallel bars where Steve, another physio, was putting John, a homeless Vietnam veteran, through his paces with his first ever prosthetic leg. Trinity had also made her way over, followed closely by Chase.

'Ready to go?' she asked, smiling at Eddie.

'Sure am.'

'You're doing well, Pops,' Reid said.

'Definitely,' Mario reiterated.

'You back on Thursday, Eddie?' Chase asked.

Eddie glanced at Mario, who nodded and said, 'Yep. We'll keep you going twice a week on the weight work. It'll help strengthen all your bones.'

Chase turned flirty eyes on Trinity and smiled at her. 'So that means you'll be back too.'

'Looks like it.'

She returned the smile but it gave Reid some measure of satisfaction that there was nothing flirtatious in the way she looked at Chase. Her demeanour was friendly, not flirty.

Eddie raised his hand and waved at John and at Shaun, who was currently struggling up a short set of wooden steps with his new prosthesis, under the supervision of another physio.

'See you later,' he called. They both acknowledged him before turning back to their tasks.

Chase held out his hand and Eddie shook it. 'Next time, man,' Chase said. Then he turned his gaze on Trinity and put on his best *hey, baby* voice. 'I hope to see you next time too.'

Trinity nodded. 'That would be nice.'

Reid suppressed a smile at her bland response. If Chase was disappointed in *nice* he didn't show it as Reid walked his grandfather and Trinity to the door.

'I'll see you at home this arvo, Pops,' he said before turning to Trinity. 'Thanks again for this. You have no idea how much I appreciate it.'

Her hair had been scraped back into her usual low ponytail at her nape, her fringe feathering her forehead. She wasn't wearing any make-up. She never wore it. Not that he thought she needed it or that women should wear it, he just didn't know any woman who *didn't* apply a little something before leaving the house.

He supposed make-up was a luxury for a woman who didn't have a house to leave.

'It's my job,' she dismissed. 'You pay me to do it.' But there was no mistaking the blush that bloomed across her cheekbones.

Interesting…who needed make-up when flushed cheeks were so damn alluring?

'I know. But it's still appreciated.'

She nodded awkwardly. 'C'mon, Eddie, let's

go home,' she said, slipping her hand under his elbow and guiding him out of the clinic.

A low wolf whistle from behind dragged Reid back into the room. He turned to find Chase grinning at him. 'Well, aren't you the lucky one, hiring Eddie Little Miss Sweet Knees as a *companion*.'

'Little Miss Sweet Knees?'

He nodded. 'I think I'm in there.'

'Oh, please,' Kathy chimed in. 'You think you're in with any woman who doesn't throw their drink over you.'

'Kathy—' Chase grabbed his chest and faked a hurt expression '—I'm a one-legged man with a fragile ego. You wound me.'

'Right,' she snorted. 'An IED straight to your ego wouldn't wound you.'

Chase threw his head back and laughed. A lot of people outside these walls might have been horrified by Kathy's seemingly insensitive dig. But this was a hard-core environment. Learning to walk again with a prosthesis was hard-core stuff and sometimes patients had to be goaded and cajoled into doing it.

Physical therapy wasn't for wimps. Their military training helped but there was still a lot of swearing and sometimes even tears. The physical therapy staff were at the coalface—they were trained to know when to push and when to back off and it wasn't uncommon for them to cop some frustrated verbal abuse.

Learning how to give as good as they got was essential.

'I'm thinking I might ask her out when I see her on Thursday,' Chase said, returning his attention to Reid. 'I...won't be stepping on any toes?'

'Since when do you come here on Thursday?'

'Since today.' Chase grinned. 'Well?'

'She doesn't *belong* to me,' Reid grouched. 'She's allowed to see whoever she wants to see.'

Chase's forehead rose at Reid's gruff reply. 'Are you sure about that, man?' he teased. 'You seem kinda pissed off.'

'Your face pisses me off,' Reid deadpanned. Smack talk, the language of the military.

'Aw, Kathy,' Chase said, turning to appeal to the woman who was measuring Brett's stump. 'Help me out here?'

'Don't look at me,' she warned, eyes on her job. 'Your face pisses me off too.'

The whole room cracked up at that.

'You do know she has a kid, right?' Reid said.

'Of course. Ollie.'

'Oscar.'

'He's four.'

Reid shoved his hands on his hips. 'He's five.'

'Right.' Chase grinned. 'Oscar. Who's five.'

'You might have to go somewhere family friendly and take him with you.'

'Aw come on, man. They're living with you—you could babysit for a night, right? You like kids, don't you?'

Reid liked kids just fine but he hardly thought that was the point. 'She might be more amenable to a guy who's willing to include her son right from the get-go, doofus.'

Did he *have* to hand Trinity to Chase on a goddamn freaking platter?

'Or maybe she's just dying to have some adult one-on-one time? You know—' He waggled his eyebrows and Reid wondered if twenty-somethings were getting dumber these days. 'Without her kid hanging around all the time.'

Reid snorted. *Good luck with that.* He'd seen her yesterday morning at breakfast trying to be upbeat about Oscar's first day of school, stoking his excitement, fussing over his uniform and encouraging his chatter even though Reid could see the emotion in her eyes when Oscar's attention was elsewhere.

As if she wanted to snatch him to her side and never let him out in the big bad world.

'Right,' Reid said. 'You should definitely go with that angle.'

He had a feeling that Trinity's heart had been taken five years ago and she was a one-guy woman.

Trinity opened the door and placed her car keys— which also now included a house key—on the hallstand at just before ten, a smile on her face. It was the last day of Oscar's second week and, so far, school had been an outstanding success. All her fears and worries about him not liking it or missing her had been put to bed and he was thriving.

There'd been a special welcome parade for the new parents this morning, which she'd stayed on for. Seeing Oscar up on stage in front of the whole school with the other new kids in his class, singing a welcome song, had filled her heart to bursting.

The sense that things really were going to be all right settled around. The thought of leaving all the difficult times behind them made her giddy and for the first time in a long time she felt as if she could breathe properly.

'Eddie?'

She'd taken some pictures of Oscar up on stage on her phone for Eddie and couldn't wait to show him. She walked into the television room where he'd been when she left. He'd been doing some Sudoku puzzles, which he loved and the hospital had recommended to help keep his brain active.

He wasn't in the living room. 'Eddie?' she called again. Maybe he was out watering the garden?

She checked outside. And in his room. And his en-suite. No Eddie.

'Eddie?'

A note of panic crept into her voice as a trickle of fear slid into her system. She checked the other downstairs bathroom, the office, even the garage. She took the stairs two at a time, calling his name as she looked frantically in all the upstairs rooms. Including Reid's, which she'd kept the hell away from thus far.

'Eddie!' The silence that roared back at her was deafening.

That breath she'd been taking was sucked away.

Where could he have got to? She remembered the thugs at the park and the hot lick of fear chilled to ice in her veins.

She bolted down the stairs, scooped the keys off the hallstand and flew out of the house. She barely looked both ways as she crossed the road, praying like crazy that Eddie had decided to feed the ducks. But there was no Eddie anywhere near the pond. Trinity jogged the length and breadth of the park calling his name, her heart hammering more from fear than exertion.

She didn't find him lying unconscious on the ground either and she couldn't decide if she was relieved or even more petrified. 'Where are you, Eddie?' she muttered.

She ran back across the street, adrenaline and bile settling uneasily like oil on water in her gut. She banged on the doors of the neighbours either side but neither of them had seen Eddie leave. She looked up and down the street, hoping to catch a glimpse of his snowy-white head but there was nothing.

It didn't stop her running up and down it though, calling his name.

God. She'd been watching over him for two weeks—two lousy weeks—and she'd already failed to do the one thing Reid had wanted her to do. Keep an eye on him.

Reid who had offered her so much.

What if Eddie had fallen down somewhere and broken his other hip? What if some other thugs had bailed him up and this time hurt him?

What if he'd had a stroke? Or a heart attack?

The possibilities mounted like boogie men in her mind and by the time she'd got back to the house with still no Eddie she knew she was going to have to call Reid and tell him she'd lost his grandfather.

CHAPTER EIGHT

'*REID?*' TRINITY WAS jogging along the footpath again, peering down the side streets, her gaze searching for Eddie's big, slightly stooped frame and wild white hair.

'What's wrong?'

His voice was low but alert in her ear and she knew instantly that *he* knew something was up. He'd have to be deaf not to pick up on the panic and distress in her voice.

'I was home later than usual…' she was puffing and panting as she ran to the frantic pound of her heart '…this morning because…' puff, puff '…there was a special welcome parade and—'

'Trinity.' He cut into her rambling. 'What's wrong? Has something happened?'

Trinity stopped jogging, the enormity of the situation pulling her to a dead stop. Her pulse washed like Niagara Falls through her ears and dread filled all the space in her chest she needed to breathe. 'Eddie's gone. I can't find him. He wasn't in the house when I got home.'

There was a long pause and Trinity wished she could see his face. Was he worried, annoyed or flat-out angry? After spending the last two weeks trying to keep some distance between them she suddenly wished he were beside her.

Even if he was angry he was a man who exuded capability as if it was God-given and she could sure as hell do with some of that right now.

'When was the last time you saw him?'

'We left for school at eight-thirty. I'm usually home by just after nine but—'

He cut her off briskly. 'Where are you now? Are you home?'

'I'm searching the side streets.'

'I'm coming now. I'll try a few of his old haunts. Go home.'

She wasn't annoyed by the order—she was pleased he was thinking methodically—but she needed to do *something*. 'I can't just sit at home. Text me some locations I can help search.'

His response was swift. 'No. I need you home in case he turns up there.'

Trinity had been all set to argue her point but she couldn't fault that logic. There was no use them both out combing the streets if Eddie had returned home.

'Okay. Sure.' She turned back for the house. 'Look, Reid… I'm so, *so* sorry.'

'It's fine, Trinity.' The briskness was gone. His voice was soft and compassionate.

'But what if he—?'

'I'll find him.'

Trinity stomped down on all the ways that Eddie could be hurt. The last thing Reid needed was her litany of worst-case scenarios when he probably had a hundred of his own.

'It'll be okay, don't worry,' he assured her. 'He can't have gone too far. Speak soon.'

The phone went dead, his assurances not helping one iota.

An hour later she got the phone call that Eddie was safe and Reid was bringing him home. Trinity groped for the steps behind her, falling back onto the third one as relief flooded her system. She'd been pacing the floor area between the internal staircase and the front door while trying and failing to keep all those thoughts stuffed down.

She'd pictured him dead and maimed in so many different ways.

Now she was dizzy with relief.

Fifteen minutes later she heard the key in the lock and all but ran to greet Eddie as he appeared, launching herself at his big frame, hugging him hard. 'Eddie! You gave me a heart attack.'

The old man caught her and laughed. 'I'm so sorry, my dear,' he said, his eyes twinkling. 'Got a call from a dear friend who was in town. Wanted to meet for a beer in the old stomping ground. I should have let Reid know what I was up to or left you a note. I just forgot...'

Trinity noted Eddie had put on some smart clothes. 'Oh. So you didn't...'

She glanced at a grinning Reid, who shook his head. 'Found him at the local pub a few kilometres away.'

So he'd just...gone out? Drinking. *At nine in the morning.* But he *hadn't* wandered away.

Well. Okay, then. Why shouldn't he? This *was* his life. His house. He'd no doubt been coming and going from it for decades without telling anyone his business. He didn't need her permission or approval. He wasn't a prisoner here and, as Reid had said, she wasn't Eddie's jailer.

Still, he'd scared a decade off her life, and, for someone who already looked more than her twenty-four years, she could do without the addition of grey hair.

'Anything to eat?' Eddie asked, cheerfully. 'Two beers on an empty stomach and I'm as dizzy as a top.'

Trinity blinked. 'Ah…sure. I'll make you a sandwich.'

'Cheese and pickle? That would be lovely,' he said, patting her on the arm before heading in the direction of the living room.

'He can make his own sandwiches,' Reid said, following her into the kitchen.

'I don't mind.'

'Doing things for him won't help keep his brain active.'

'I'm making him one lousy cheese and pickle sandwich,' Trinity chided. She'd have gone out and slain a deer if he'd asked for venison. 'He can make his own tomorrow.'

She dragged the bread, butter and cheese out of the fridge and dumped them on the bench. Her hands shook as reaction to Eddie being safe set in. She grabbed the pickles from the pantry but the adrenaline that had maintained her in a state of high alert chose that moment to drain away in an almost audible *whoosh*.

Eddie was safe. He hadn't had a stroke, broken his hip again or been attacked. Her legs wobbled and the jar fell from suddenly nerveless fingers, smashing on the floor.

She swore under her breath, staring at the pile of glass and the ooze of thick yellow pickles as she knelt to clean it up.

Reid leapt to her aid, grabbing a roll of paper towel off the bench as he crouched beside the mess. 'Be careful, don't cut yourself.'

The adrenaline surge had left her wrung out and irritable. His broad shoulders seemed to loom over her. His thighs, clad in his bike leathers, seemed to loom up at her. And his feet looked huge in his big biker boots.

'Gee thanks,' she muttered as she picked out the larger pieces of glass from the spilled food, placing them on a paper towel he thrust at her. 'I was planning on doing just that.'

Did he think she was stupid?

He ignored her sarcasm and they worked together, her kneeling, him crouching, his big boots and spread thighs in her direct line of vision.

'I'll get the mop,' she said, once the mess was taken care of.

'No need.' He departed momentarily before

crouching down again with a thick wad of wet paper towels. 'A spot-mop'll do. The cleaner will be here tomorrow morning.'

Oh, yes. *The cleaner.* Trinity had never known such luxury. In fact, she'd usually been *the cleaner.*

He went to do the job but she wrested the paper towel off him. He didn't resist too hard, which saved a dumb tug-of-war. She was hyperaware, though, of him watching her as she swiped the stickiness away. Conscious of his nearness. Of the way he filled out his bike leathers and the battered state of his sturdy boots.

'Looks good,' he said, once she'd thoroughly swabbed the area.

Trinity glanced at him. *He was so close.* She didn't think she'd ever been this close—for good reason. She could see the individual golden brown strands of his beard and smell the aftershave he wore so damn well. Her heart rate picked up again but for an entirely different reason than a missing grandfather.

God, what was she doing down here on the floor with him?

She'd already dragged him away from his work and caused him who knew how much stress over his pop and now he was cleaning up another mess of hers.

She needed to apologise and send him back to work.

'Look… I'm *so* sorry for dragging you out of work like that. I just assumed that he'd wandered away and I panicked. I didn't even consider that he might have left with an actual purpose in mind.'

'It's fine,' Reid assured her. 'I assumed the same thing. And I want you to ring me if you ever have any concerns about Pops. Any time, okay?'

She nodded, the movement of his mouth distracting. She liked the way it sat in amongst his facial hair, the whiskers perfectly groomed to delineate the margins of his lips. She wanted to run her fingers around his mouth and feel the tickle of whiskers against the pads of her finger and the contrasting softness of his lips.

He'd gone very still all of a sudden and her breath hitched as his gaze dropped to *her* mouth.

Oh, Lordy!

'Thank you…for coming.' It was just for something to say but she instantly regretted it when his mouth kicked up at one corner in wicked suggestion. Trinity blushed under the steady heat of his gaze.

'For leaving work,' she clarified quickly. 'For dropping everything. Just…thank you. And thank you *a hundred times* for finding him.'

God, yes. Definitely that. Seeing Eddie again had been such a relief.

He smiled at her and it was so damn sexy she was lost to the pull of his mouth. She'd never kissed a man with a beard. The fact that this man was highly inappropriate didn't seem to matter right now.

'You should get back to work,' she said in an effort to distract herself from the potency of his attraction and the tug of her hormones.

He nodded but didn't move and before she could check the impulse she leaned forward and pressed her lips to his.

That was it. Just a press. A tentative thing. Shy, almost. No opening of lips, no angling of heads to accommodate noses, no aligning of bodies, no sigh as they settled in.

Just her lips on his.

Testing, trying.

His whiskers spiked pleasantly at the outline of her mouth, his scent teased her nostrils and the husky timbre of his breathing tickled her ears. Time suspended in that moment or two before a kiss became *something else*.

And then common sense rushed in and she pulled back as if she'd been zapped, her tripping pulse stuttering to a momentary halt as shock set in. She stared at Reid, aghast, her hand covering her mouth as he stared too.

'I...' She removed her hand in the hopes she'd say something sensible, something to justify her completely inexcusable actions. She'd *kissed* him, for crying out loud.

'I...'

Nothing. She had nothing. She couldn't think above the bang of her restarted heart fibrillating through her ribcage. But she had to say *something*.

'I'm so...*so* sorry,' she stuttered, her gaze glued to his face with its completely inscrutable expression. 'That was *completely* and *utterly* inappropriate. I don't know—'

'Trinity.'

Her pulse leapt at his interruption but she ignored him. 'What came over me. I was just so... scared—'

'Trinity.'

'That something had happened,' she said, ploughing on, needing to get an apology out before she dissolved in a nervous puddle, 'to Eddie and to see he was okay—'

She cut out as he dropped from a crouch to a kneel bringing him *so much closer*. So close their thighs almost touched and she could feel the warm fan of his breath on her cheek. Her body stiffened and her heart raced as a crazy buzz started up deep inside her pelvis. She eased her torso back, putting some distance between them.

'To…to…to *know* he was okay,' she said, ignoring the dryness of her mouth as she forced herself to continue, 'and to see him come through that door with you—'

'Trinity,' Reid said, interrupting her again, sliding a hand onto the side of her neck before slipping it all the way around to her nape.

'What?'

Her voice, low and husky, was barely audible as his hand urged her closer, her body aligning with his. His lips were just there, the bristles of his beard were just there and she curled her fingers into her palms to stop herself from touching. Her skin sizzled wherever his body made contact with hers.

'Be quiet,' he muttered and brought his mouth down on hers.

There was nothing shy about *this* kiss.

It was open-mouthed from the start. Nothing *pleasant* about the tickle of his whiskers. They scraped erotically against her chin and cheeks as he angled his head to deepen the kiss, prickling in a tidal wave of sensation down her entire body, hardening her nipples and settling right between her legs.

His scent *raged* like a juggernaut through her system. His breathing was the harsh suck of a hurricane in her ears. Her pulse didn't *trip*, it *pounded* like a jackhammer through her head and chest and all her pulse points.

Reid was a full-body experience and she was utterly consumed by the havoc he was wreaking.

And his tongue. God, his tongue. Swiping and thrusting and stroking. Thick and urgent as it explored and demanded hers do the same in return. It tore whimpers from her throat and weakened her knees. If she hadn't already threaded her fingers through his belt loops she'd have slumped to the floor at the first touch of his tongue.

It had been a long time since someone had kissed her. And *never* like this. Brian's kisses paled by comparison. He'd kissed her like the seventeen-year-old he'd been. They'd taught each other, fumbling their way through the joys of sex but too often constrained by lack of privacy. Doss houses and homeless communities, where people all huddled together for warmth and security under whatever bridge or shelter they could, were not conducive to long, lazy days of sexual exploration.

Bri had kissed like a teenager learning the ropes. Reid kissed like a fully grown man.

Like a master.

Like a grand freaking wizard.

'How's that sandwich coming along?'

Eddie's voice came from somewhere out in the hall but it had a galvanising effect. They sprang apart and were on their feet by the time Eddie poked his head into the kitchen.

'Sorry, Eddie, just dropped the pickles,' Trinity said, her pulse fluttering madly, her face hot as she blindly grabbed two slices of bread out of the packet and started buttering.

'We usually keep more than one jar,' Reid said, heading for the pantry. 'I'll get it.'

'No!' Her knife clattered to the bench.

Reid stopped and Eddie blinked at her vehemence. 'You need to be getting back to work.' She forced herself to look at him but all she could see was his lips, a dark, dusky red from their kisses. 'I can get the damn pickles.'

Their eyes met and held for long moments before his gaze dropped to her mouth too.

'She's right, Reid,' Eddie said, completely oblivious to the highway of crackling electricity arcing between them. 'You really should be at work.'

He dragged his gaze off her and smiled at his grandfather. 'Sure thing, Pops. I'll see you some time after two. No more slipping out for beers without telling Trinity first, okay?'

Eddie chuckled. 'I promise.'

Trinity was aware of Reid switching his attention to her. Aware in the same kind of way she'd been aware of him since the day she'd met him. She didn't need to look at him to feel it. Hell, she could have been totally blind and she'd have felt it.

'See you later, Trinity.'

She wasn't sure whether it was a statement of fact or some kind of illicit promise but she was damned if she was going to clarify it. 'Yep,' she said, refusing to look up from the job at hand.

She sensed his gaze on her, hot and heavy for long moments before he clapped his grandfather on the back and exited the kitchen.

It was only then Trinity dared breathe deeply again.

CHAPTER NINE

REID COULDN'T CONCENTRATE on work once he returned. Trinity had done the right thing ringing him and his grandfather was safe at home but Pops' cheeky pint at the pub with his mates was not what occupied his brain.

It should be. Trying to balance his grandfather's rights to an autonomous, dignified life with the need to keep him safe was going to present all kinds of future challenges if the drug trial wasn't successful and he started to deteriorate. But all he could think about this afternoon was that kiss.

Both of them.

Even her first chaste kiss played on a loop in his head. So innocent compared to the next one but just as sexy.

He couldn't remember ever being kissed by a woman like that. Most women who took the initiative usually went in with all guns blazing. Open mouths. A lot of tongue. Squashing themselves up against him, squirming deliciously, raking their hands into his hair and moaning his name.

Trinity hadn't done any of those things. It had been a closed-mouth, very still, very silent kiss. Yet it was probably one of the sweetest kisses that had ever been laid on his mouth.

It had turned him on more than any kiss he could ever remember.

Frankly he was a fan of all types of kissing but this one had reminded him a bit of his first. Starting off simple, not daring to move or get too fancy in case he'd screw it up even as his body yearned for more.

Yearning.

He'd seen that in Trinity's eyes just prior to her making her move. As if she couldn't stop herself. As if she couldn't *deny* herself. The knowledge had flared through his system like a lit match and still buzzed through him a couple of hours later.

Reid tried to drag his attention back to the report he was writing for the hospital board on partnering with a robotics lab going into the future but he couldn't stop thinking about Trinity.

About where they went from here.

It was clear she'd been embarrassed at the prospect of being caught kissing him. Although, in all truth, by the time Pops came along *he* was kissing her.

She might have started it but he'd definitely finished it.

Hell, he hadn't been any too pleased at the prospect of being sprung by his grandfather either. He wasn't some fifteen-year-old kid any more and he'd rather not flaunt whatever it was that was happening between him and Trinity when it was something he wasn't exactly proud of. He'd been trying since she'd arrived at his place not to think of her in any kind of sexual way but he couldn't deny he was attracted to her.

He just wished he knew why.

A life in the military hadn't been conducive to forming long-term relationships but a man didn't get to thirty-four without female companionship. He guessed he had a *type* and it wasn't Trinity. Women who were flirty and witty and easy to be around. Who were relaxed and could hold a conversation in a room full of army officers or laugh at a dirty joke. Hell, *tell* a dirty joke. Who were confident in themselves and their bodies and their sex appeal.

Trinity was none of those things.

She was quiet and unassuming. Wary. Contained. Prickly, more often than not. Slow to trust. If anything she hid her sex appeal beneath ill-fitting clothes and a wall of polite indifference that could morph to out-and-out hostility.

He understood why. She was a single mother with a young son who'd been doing it tough for a long time. She didn't have time for the frivolities of life. She was working her fingers to the bone just to survive. Her son was her priority— not herself.

And he admired the hell out of her for that.

But since when had he found it sexually attractive? Because there was something about her that definitely piqued his interest. That didn't just pull at his heart strings but at the ones in his groin too.

Maybe it was her resilience. Her…gumption. It was the word that had popped into his head the first day they'd met and it'd stuck. He'd always admired gumption—in anyone. But Trinity wore it better than anyone he knew.

Who knew that could be so damn sexy?

Maybe it was the fact it had been a long time between drinks for him? He'd had a couple of one-night stands when he'd been on the road. Women he'd met along the way. Fellow travellers.

Maybe it was some weird misplaced, macho,

protection thing left over from the military. But Trinity had already demonstrated she didn't need his protection.

Whatever it was, it was a problem because he'd been thinking about kissing her a lot this past couple of weeks. It was that mouth. The fullness, the lushness. For a woman who made nothing of her features, it drew his gaze like moth to flame.

But he hadn't acted on it. The power dynamic between them sucked and he did not want to be *that* guy.

He *wasn't* that guy.

Until today. When he'd thrown his moral high ground right out of the window.

Her kissing him was one thing. But him kissing her? *Taking over?* That was a whole other *thing*. She hadn't even been able to look at him after so he'd no doubt destroyed any kind of fragile trust they'd been building this past couple of weeks. And that wouldn't do. He'd been trying to show her that there were good people out there, that she could trust people.

That she could trust *him*.

So he was going to have to rein himself in because what he wanted here didn't matter. She wasn't the kind of woman that would indulge in a fling and even suggesting something like that to someone in her position was completely abhorrent to him.

He would never put her in that kind of situation.

Trinity and Oscar were with them temporarily. Until she got back on her feet. He was giving her *breathing space*. The last thing she needed was him *breathing down her neck*.

Another guy she couldn't trust.

So kissing Trinity was out. No matter how damn much he wanted to.

Trinity came home from school pickup sans Oscar the following Friday. It was strange to be without him. They'd rarely ever been apart and she was feeling stupidly fragile.

It was so *dumb*. It was what she wanted for him. She just hadn't realised how hard it was going to be.

'Where's the little dude?' Reid asked when she wandered into the kitchen. He was making a giant sandwich.

Of course.

The man was always eating.

Facing him again after their kiss had been awkward to say the least, even a week later. Facing him in the *kitchen*—the scene of the crime—was especially awkward.

By tacit agreement, neither of them had mentioned the kiss. Trinity figured the less attention that was drawn to it, the quicker it would be to forget. Re-establishing the distance that had been eroded between them had helped too. Keeping herself aloof from him both physically and conversationally had given her back some control.

Now if only she could control what went on in her head when she shut her eyes. A series of very hot dreams about *way* more intimate things than kissing had left her tired and achy in places that hadn't ached in a long time.

She might have actually blushed at the thought as she faced him now but she was battling other emotions. 'He's gone on a play date to Raymond's house.'

Her son had a friend.

The words were foreign and her voice sounded wobbly so she cleared her throat. This was a *good* thing. It was exactly what she'd hoped for when Oscar went to school. That he'd make friends and finally have a normal life.

'Oh. That's *great*,' Reid said. His gorgeous face

cracked wide open; he was obviously chuffed at the news, his blue eyes shining.

'Yes.' She nodded, swallowing the massive lump in her throat. It *was* awesome. It was beyond her wildest dreams.

So why then was she about to burst into tears?

The tears she'd been battling all the way home prickled in her nose and burned all the way along her sinuses. They pushed at her tear ducts, threatening imminent appearance. They'd been threatening since Celia, Raymond's mother, had approached and asked if it was okay for Oscar to come over for a few hours.

Trinity had met Celia and Raymond the first day. She'd liked the other woman instantly and they'd chatted outside the classroom most days waiting to pick the kids up in the afternoon. And Oscar had talked about Raymond non-stop.

He'd been barely able to contain his excitement and had wrapped his skinny arms hard around her neck when Trinity had said yes to the play date. Watching him skip away, hand in hand with Raymond, had been the most beautiful thing she'd ever witnessed.

And the hardest.

'She's dropping Oscar home at five on their way to Raymond's swimming lesson.'

'Cool. Do him good to mix with some people his own age for a change.'

Reid munched on his sandwich oblivious to Trinity's inner turmoil. She knew he wasn't criticising her but she wasn't feeling particularly strong at the moment.

Goddamn it. She could count on one hand the number of times she'd cried these last five years and they'd all been at Oscar's hospital bed when things had seemed utterly hopeless.

She hadn't even cried when she'd found out Brian had died. She'd had a premmie baby with a serious heart condition on life support. There hadn't been any spare emotional energy for someone she'd left months beforehand and who hadn't wanted his child anyway.

But she'd been in this house for three weeks and she'd almost cried a dozen bloody times. And now she really *was* going to cry.

But not in front of Reid.

'Will you excuse me?' she said, a smile fixed on her face as she turned and walked out of the room.

She walked to the stairs, her sinuses burning

from suppressing the well of emotion. Once she got to them she took them two by two, hurrying to her room, desperate to be tucked away inside when the well overflowed.

She shut the door behind her, her heart racing, silent tears falling down her cheeks now. Oscar's old, floppy bunny sat in the middle of his pillow and the threatening tears burst like a dam.

She tried to choke them back as she curled up on the bed, bunny clutched to her chest. She tried to tell herself this was stupid and futile and embarrassing. That Oscar was happy. But she'd been so worried about him. About him not making friends or fitting in. About being teased because he was smaller.

And now he had a friend.

And it was wonderful and she was so happy she couldn't stop crying. She tried to muffle her weeping, burying her face in his rabbit, but inhaling the smells of Oscar—the baby powder he still liked to wear after his bath and the orange blossom from the cheap-as-chips shampoo he loved so much—only made it worse.

She didn't hear the knock on the door and, facing away from it, she didn't see it open but she *sensed* Reid's presence the way she always did. 'Trinity.'

It was quiet and tentative, causing another well of emotion in her chest, and she shut her eyes hard against it as she suppressed a rising sob.

'Go away.' There was no way to disguise the sniffles or her voice, cracked and husky with emotion.

'Trinity.'

'God, please, just…go away,' she half cried, half begged. Trinity didn't have much in the world but her dignity and she didn't want Reid to see her like this.

There was a hesitation then a quiet, 'No.'

She sensed him coming closer and swallowed a painful lump. *Bloody hell, Reid!* She sucked in a husky breath, dashing the tears away with her hands as she rolled over to face him.

'I'm fine,' she said, her voice rough and low.

He was standing about a foot away from the bed, a line creasing his brows together, blue eyes telegraphing their concern and helplessness. He was in usual jeans and T-shirt and stood, hands on hips, looking down at her. Between the broad set of his shoulders and the tattoos on his arms he seemed to take up all the space in the room.

Trinity swung her legs over the side of the bed, levering herself upright. It was bad enough he was witnessing her crying for Australia, she didn't want him looming over her as well.

He cocked an eyebrow. 'You don't look fine. Are you worried about this Raymond kid? Do you think Oscar's not safe?'

'Of course not,' she snapped. 'Do you think I'd let Oscar go and play somewhere I didn't think he'd be *safe*?'

'No. Absolutely not...sorry.' He shoved a hand through his hair. 'But something's obviously upset you. Why else would you be crying?'

She had no idea why, seconds after being annoyed with him, tears swamped her vision and her face was crumpling again. 'Because I'm h... happy,' she choked out, a wave of emotion rolling through her body.

'Oh, God.' He searched her face, looking even more helpless, putting a hand out as if to reach for her then thinking better of it, shoving it on his hip. 'Please...don't cry.'

The statement and the distress in his voice surprised her. Where she'd grown up most men had been impervious to crying women.

'Look... *God*...don't, okay?' He took a step towards her then stopped, raked his hand through his hair again, hesitated another moment then covered the short distance between them and sat next to her on the bed, leaving a space big enough for Oscar to have sat between them.

His denim-clad thighs were big compared to the bared slimness of hers. Her baggy shorts had ridden up to reveal a lot of leg. If she'd been in her right mind she might have cared.

'It's okay,' he repeated, awkwardly sliding a hand around her shoulders, patting her arm absently while scrupulously maintaining their distance.

Trinity was too much of an emotional wreck to pay any heed to her determination to keep a physical distance between them. His arm around her felt *so* good, she actually leaned into him, put her head on his shoulder.

It was a novelty to have someone comforting her. She was so used to wading through the ups and downs of life solo it was a new experience to *not* be alone.

She'd been too afraid in the past that any sign of fragility would be a signal to those in charge that she wasn't coping. Too afraid that deeper questions would be asked. That the prying into her *circumstances* would begin.

It was different with Reid. While she was wary of her physical attraction to him, it was liberating to realise he already *knew* her deepest secret. She could let it all out with him and not worry about the consequences, just soak up how good it felt to lean on a man for a change.

'I don't know why I'm crying,' she said, sniffling loudly as she lifted her head, her gaze fixing on his as well as it could through a tsunami of tears. 'I *never* cry.'

'Yeah.' He inched closer until their thighs were touching and her head was more supported. He urged it back on his shoulder. 'That's probably why.'

His hand was warm, his palm gently rubbing up and down her arm. 'I'm just so h...happy he has a friend,' she said, more tears squeezing out around closed lids. 'I've been so excited for him but I just didn't expect to m...miss him so much.'

She couldn't go on, dissolving into tears again.

He rubbed her arm some more and dropped a kiss on top of her head. It didn't seem strange, it felt *right*.

He held her like that for a long time until her

tears stopped and the weeping faded to the odd hiccoughy sobs.

'If it's any consolation,' he murmured, somewhere above her head as she quieted, 'I don't think you're the first mother to find letting their kid go emotionally challenging.'

The word's rumbled through his ribcage. Trinity heard them through the wall of his chest where her ear was half pressed.

'I suppose not,' she said with a wry smile as she glanced at him. 'If only my parents could see me now. Not much of the *Matrix* Trinity about me today, huh?'

'Tough guys have their low moments too. It's how they keep getting up again that has us rooting for them.'

He smiled down at her and kissed her forehead this time and Trinity felt so much better. So damn good and comforted.

For the first time in her life she actually felt she had someone on her side. Someone rooting for her.

'Thank you,' she whispered. And then they were both smiling at each other.

CHAPTER TEN

TRINITY WASN'T SURE who kissed who. All she knew was their mouths fitted together perfectly and it was *just* what the doctor ordered. His warm, male scent swirled around her like fairy dust, his chest was hard and his heart beat a steady thump beneath her palms and she wanted more.

So much more.

He pulled away though and she moaned in protest.

'Trinity…'

The look in his eyes was raw and untamed and her breath hitched. With only one lover to her name, Trinity was no expert in this kind of thing. But she did recognise the potency of desire, could see it in someone else.

'Reid,' she whispered.

She opened to him as he came back for more on a strangled groan, her pulse roaring in her ears, her senses filling with the warm, heady scent of him. The bristles of his beard prickled at her mouth and she whimpered against his lips as the sensation headed south, hitting all her *good* spots.

Her throat. Her nipples. Deep inside her belly. The nerve endings at the base of her spine. Between her legs.

Her body burned for him, slick and achy.

She jammed her hands in his hair, turning to press herself more fully against him, needing to be closer, to feel all of him, to touch all of him. Keeping her lips locked with his, she slid her hands over his shoulders and her leg over his lap, turning until she was straddling him.

He groaned again, breaking away. 'Trinity...'

His voice was a crazy low rumble as they stared at each other, chests heaving, their mouths wet. She was speechless in the presence of her desire. She didn't know how to ask for what she wanted. How to articulate herself in the presence of his intoxicating masculinity. His denim-clad quads rubbed deliciously against the sensitive flesh of her inner thighs, his taste flooded her tongue and his scent filled her nostrils.

They shouldn't be doing this, she knew, yet she was hungry for the physical contact. *Starving.* For this man to lose herself in.

She grabbed at the shoulder muscles beneath

her palms and pushed him back. He didn't resist, going down at her insistence, his tattooed arms loose by his sides, his hips pressing warm and firm against the inside of each knee. He didn't say anything for long moments, just searched her gaze, his chest chugging air in and out as their gazes locked and blood throbbed at her temples.

Then he lifted his head and lunged for her mouth. Trinity gasped as their lips made contact, moaning long and loud as she accepted the almost brutal demand of his mouth. She followed his head back down, their mouths fused as his hands slid up the backs of her thighs to her butt. He squeezed and yanked her down to him.

She went willingly, her body collapsing on top of his, aligning perfectly as he urged her thighs apart, splaying wide over the bulge behind his fly, one big hand holding her fast right where it felt best.

Reid could barely think as his senses infused with the taste and smell and the sounds of Trinity *indulging*. Panting and gasping as their heads twisted and turned, their tongues duelling, stoking the passion between them as she rocked and grinded on top of him.

He shoved a hand into her hair at her nape, pressing her mouth closer and harder at the same time he pressed her hips closer and harder. The rub of her pelvis against the taut line of his erection was almost painful but there was something to be said for hurting so good and he wanted every inch of her along every inch of him.

There was no coherence of strategy. Just feeling and moving and instinct. Going with what was good. And damned if her hot, deep kisses didn't *taste* good. And if the little noises at the back of her throat didn't *sound* good. And if the rock of her pelvis over his didn't *feel* good.

Really freaking good.

She gasped, wrenching her mouth from his, throwing her head back, her eyes squeezed shut, her neck bare and exposed and right there. The look of ecstasy on her face was like a shot of testosterone to his already overloaded system and he ground up hard against her as he nuzzled her neck.

'Feels good, huh?' he said, keeping up the grind as he deliberately scraped his whiskers across the pale, delicate skin of her throat.

Her eyes flew open on another gasp, her gaze

fixing on his, her tawny eyes wide, turning dark as whiskey. 'I'm coming,' she moaned.

Reid blinked. *She was what now?*

The sudden violent arch of her back and the intense trembling of her arms bracketing his shoulders confirmed it.

'Oh, God…oh, God…*oh, God*!' she gasped, her eyes screwed shut, drumming the flats of her feet against the mattress either side of his hips as she rode him and the powerful wave of her orgasm.

Reid's chest pounded as he held her through it but it was like the bucket of proverbial cold water. She was oblivious to his stillness as she got off on him. She didn't need him to do anything, she was taking what she wanted—what she obviously *needed*—grinding hard against him, gasping and panting and wringing every single second out of her climax.

He wouldn't have denied her a few moments of sexual abandon for the world. For God's sake, the woman was so starved of sex and human *affection* that she'd just come fully clothed from a spot of dry humping.

But it should *not* have been with him.

What the hell had he done? Where the hell had his resolve to keep away from her gone?

Because, regardless of how much he'd wanted her, she was still a poor, highly vulnerable single mother and he was a well-off guy who was offering refuge and paying her to look after his grandfather.

And he'd gone and taken advantage of her situation. Or at least let things get out of control. Not much better than the douchebag who'd demanded sex in turn for accommodation.

Where the hell was his *honour*?

With one last moan and still oblivious to Reid's turmoil, she collapsed on top of him, gasping and shuddering, her fingers curled into the balls of his shoulders.

His hands automatically slid to her back, cradling her as the pound of her heart reverberated through her ribcage. Her weight against him was hardly anything at all but the weight on his conscience was significant.

He lay there, *his* heart also pounding but not from exertion, from uncertainty. He didn't want to mess with her bliss. God knew if anyone deserved a bit of bliss it was her. But he doubted she was going to be too pleased at what had occurred between them when the bliss wore off.

Ever since the kiss in the kitchen she'd been all sparks and prickles. Like an electric hedgehog.

If he knew Trinity at all after three weeks in her company, he knew there were bound to be regrets after this little *tête-à-tête*.

She stirred, lifted her head and looked at him, although both actions appeared to take a supreme effort, as did keeping her head upright. A very satisfied, Mona Lisa smile played on her mouth and slugged him straight in the heart.

There was nothing more satisfying, as a man, than putting *that* look on a woman's face.

He watched though as her gaze became clearer. She frowned at him, tentatively touching her finger to the tense line of his mouth. 'What's wrong?'

The pad of her finger was like an erotic brand and Reid fought the urge to suck it into his mouth.

She searched his face some more. 'Oh, God, I'm sorry.' She planted an elbow on his chest, levering herself up some more. 'I just…got off and left you hanging and—' She halted abruptly and slid her hand between their bodies.

'Let me…'

Her hand cupping him, still hard and throbbing despite his mental self-flagellation, had a galvanising effect.

'*Ooo*kay. No.'

He rolled her off him and practically fell from the bed in his haste to put some distance between them, adjusting himself as he went. He stopped just short of the door and turned to face her.

Slowly she rose into a sitting position. Her beautiful full mouth was a deep red from the plunder of *his* mouth. Her too-big T-shirt had slipped off one shoulder. 'I guess we stepped over the line, huh?' she said, her cheeks almost as red as her mouth.

'You could say that.'

She pushed a hand through her hair. 'I'm sorry.'

'No.' He shook his head. 'It was as much my fault.'

The kiss had come out of nowhere, sure, but maybe it had been inevitable the second he'd sat on the bed with her and put his arm around her. He should have known he was vulnerable to her.

To her situation. And her gumption. And her damn mouth.

But that was no excuse to let things get out of hand.

'I was a wreck, Reid. You were just trying to

comfort me. Put it down to…extraordinary circumstances.'

'You were *crying*, Trinity. Stop the press.'

'Trust me, for me that *is* extraordinary.'

Reid laughed at her self-deprecation. 'Crying is good for you.' He suspected she needed to do it more often.

'Oh, yeah?'

'Yes, ma'am.' He grinned. 'I learned that in med school.'

She lifted an eyebrow at him. 'You do it a lot, do you?'

'Every night. Twice on Sundays.'

She laughed and Reid's breath hitched. She laughed so little it made the times she did that much more memorable.

At least the atmosphere was a little lighter now.

'We can't do that again,' Reid said. 'Overstep the line. I'm not some creep who opens up his home with some sick ulterior motive. That's not the arrangement here.'

'I know that,' she said quietly.

'I think it's best if we keep things…platonic.' He was a grown-ass man, he could keep this attraction in check, surely?

She nodded. 'I agree.'

'I want you to be able to trust me.'

'I do trust you. I know I've been…wary. And distant. I know I don't trust easily and that's a hard habit to break. Especially when something too good to be true happens. But I *do* know you're a good guy.'

Well, well, despite the awkwardness of the situation it looked as if they'd made some kind of breakthrough. Maybe they should have had almost-sex two weeks ago.

'Does this mean you're going to stop looking at me like I might just shove you and Oscar in the oven at any moment?'

She laughed. 'Sure.'

Considering what had just gone down between them, Reid was relieved by the outcome. 'I like to think we could be friends,' he ventured.

It was a tentative suggestion—not one he was sure she'd go for—but it made sense. Putting Trinity in the friend zone and vice versa, establishing that kind of rock-solid boundary between them, should help keep the attraction at bay.

'I'd like that.'

'Let's start over.' He strode towards her, sticking his hand out to be shaken. 'Welcome, friend.'

She took his hand and shook briefly. 'Thank you.'

A weird tingle flared to life as their palms pressed together. Reid ignored it.

Friends *did not* suffer from weird tingles.

The weeks flew by and it was mid-November before Trinity knew it. Her relationship with Reid had become easier, more relaxed, as he'd hoped for that day she'd totally lost her mind and had the world's fastest orgasm. They'd both put extraordinary effort into it and it didn't feel awkward or fraught between them any more.

It felt as if she'd finally been able to take that breath and relax.

Sure, her attraction was still there. She still dreamed inappropriate dreams about him that woke her in the middle of the night with his name on her lips and an ache between her legs. And she spent an extraordinary amount of time reliving that unorthodox climax he'd given her—or rather, *she'd taken*—despite the fact her cheeks flamed every single time.

But that was a first world problem if ever there was one. She could live with it.

Not that she'd have to for much longer. By her calculations, she'd have enough money put aside in two weeks to start contacting real-estate agencies about an apartment to rent.

They'd be in their own place by Christmas.

'Hey.'

Trinity startled. She'd been so caught up in her thoughts and memories, she hadn't sensed Reid approach and she *always* sensed him approaching.

It was like some really screwed-up super power.

'Hey, Reid.' Eddie grinned as Reid shrugged out of his jacket and threw it around the back of the folding chair that had been set up for him beside his grandfather.

'Hi,' she said. He nodded but she couldn't see his eyes from the sunglasses fixed firmly on his face.

'What's the score?' he asked, turning his attention to the match being played out in the centre.

'Four for twenty-six,' Eddie said. 'Oscar's batting. He's on three.'

Eddie and Reid had accompanied her to every one of Oscar's Saturday school cricket fixtures. Reid didn't show till after work but he hadn't missed a match. Considering the truly terrible calibre of cricket on display *that* was dedication. Untrained five-and six-year-olds had no bat-and-ball skills to speak of. But, they *were* getting better and Eddie and Reid sat and cheered and supported regardless.

And Oscar loved having them amongst the spectators.

'God, it's hot,' Reid said, reaching into the Esky between the two chairs and pulling out a chilled bottle of water.

Neither she nor Eddie bothered to respond. November in Australia might be spring but it was still *painfully hot*. They, along with the other parent supporters dotted around the ground, had staked out a spot under an overhang of some gum trees. But the shady patch was retreating at a rate of knots as the sun blazed directly above them.

It was *stinking* hot.

Trinity had worried about Oscar playing in such conditions, that he didn't have the stamina for it. But he'd taken to it like a duck to water, giving her hope that he truly was over the worst of his ill health.

Suddenly a crack rent the hot, still air and the ball, smacked by Oscar, hurtled along the ground towards the boundary rope. Eddie and Reid whooped and jumped to their feet as a member of the opposing team chased the ball trying to prevent it from becoming a four. Trinity leapt up as well.

'Run,' Eddie yelled at the two stationary boys in the middle who were both staring at it as if they couldn't quite believe what had happened.

It was the first time any of them had hit the ball well and Trinity's heart burst with pride. 'Go, Oscar,' she cheered as the boys put their heads down and ran like the blazes.

They need not have though; the ball reached the boundary and the umpire signalled four runs. Reid cupped his hands around his face and called out, 'Awesome work, Oscar.'

Oscar turned, shot Reid the thumbs up and grinned so big, Trinity thought his face was going to split in two. Her lungs suddenly felt too large for her chest and Trinity was glad she was wearing sunnies too.

Her son had blossomed under the influence of the Hamilton men. *Particularly Reid.* Oscar always stood a foot taller whenever Reid praised him and constantly sought his approval.

'Phew,' Reid said as he sat again, pulling his T-shirt off his abdomen and fanning it. Trinity found her gaze was drawn helplessly to the action, knowing how firm and flat those abs were, and she was pleased for the presence of her sunglasses.

'This heat is ridiculous,' he announced.

Trinity couldn't agree more. She supposed wearing long leather bike pants and big boots made things about a hundred times worse for Reid. At least she was in shorts. Her gaze was drawn to where his fingers fanned his shirt.

Surely *no* shirt would be cooler?

'What say we head to Bondi after this?' he said suddenly, glancing at her. She looked swiftly away, hoping like hell he hadn't caught her ogling his abs.

'Go for a refreshing dip in the ocean? We can get some fish and chips for tea to celebrate that magnificent four. Would Oscar like that?'

Trinity blinked away a hot rush of tears. It seemed once you let the damn things flow you couldn't turn the suckers off. 'Oscar would love it.'

CHAPTER ELEVEN

THE ENDLESS BLUE arc of the sky met the deep blue of the Pacific Ocean at the distant horizon. The brilliant yellow of sun and sand was dazzling to the eye and even at four in the afternoon the soft grains were still warm beneath her feet. The breakers were rolling in and a line of surfers sat on their boards further out.

Red and yellow flags flapped in the stiffening afternoon breeze and surf lifesavers in their yellow shirts and red bathers with *Bondi* emblazoned across the butt patrolled the flagged area.

Trinity never got sick of this sight.

She and Oscar came to Sydney's beaches often. It cost nothing, after all, and building sandcastles and paddling in the shallows where you could easily spot a movie star frolicking in the surf was a fabulous way to forget they were part of the have nots.

They grabbed a section of sand a few metres back from where the waves washed up.

'Can we go in, Mummy?' Oscar said, bouncing on his heels as he stared at the water. He was in a full-length rasher shirt and a pair of boardies that both hung on his skinny frame.

She'd already crammed a hat on his head, lathered his arms and legs in factor fifty and slapped thick, white zinc on his face. 'Yep. Hang ten,' she said. 'Let me just slip, slop, slap too.'

'I can take him while you get ready.'

Trinity glanced up at Reid, who'd peeled down to his boardies. Her mouth dried at the sight of him. As if all the sand on the beach were suddenly in her mouth. She'd seen him without a shirt before but looking all the way up his body like this was something else entirely.

Up his tanned legs encased in pink and purple hibiscus boardies to his flat abs and further to his bronzed shoulders. His tats were in full vibrant colour beneath the spotlight of the sun. The man was tanned, ripped and built.

He was goddamn perfect.

She swore she heard a passing woman sigh at the sight of him.

'Oh…it's okay.' She swallowed. 'Thanks…but we usually just play in the sand and paddle in the shallows.'

He shrugged. 'I can do that. C'mon, little dude.' He held his hand out to Oscar, who took it without hesitation. She opened her mouth to protest but the two of them were already on their way.

'He'll take good care of the little fella,' Eddie assured her.

She nodded but it didn't stop her heartbeat echoing in her head as she tracked their progress. The tall, tattooed man with the pale, skinny kid. Oscar had to walk three paces to Reid's one but his little hand, placed so trustfully in Reid's giant one, caused her heart to squeeze painfully in Trinity's chest.

They stopped at the point where the water pushed high on the beach, foaming to a stop before retreating again. They sat and started piling up wet sand.

'I think they'll be needing these,' Eddie mused as he scooped up a couple of bright plastic buckets and spades he'd found in the shed and trotted off to join them.

Soon Eddie was crouching beside them and Oscar and Reid were on their knees digging in the sand with the spades. A lump the size of Sydney Harbour lodged in her throat at the sight of their three heads together.

Apart from the obvious differences in size and colouring, they could be a family. Father, son and grandfather out for a day at the beach.

This was what Oscar was missing out on. What Trinity couldn't give him.

A family.

Just then Oscar looked back over his shoulder, his hat lopsided on his head, his gaze searching her out, grinning and waving as he located her. He motioned to her to join them and Trinity's chest almost burst with how much she loved him.

She and Oscar *were* a family. And that was enough. She waved and rose to join her son down at the water.

'Look, Mummy, we're making a *super* castle!' Oscar announced as she drew level.

Trinity laughed and said, 'That's super-duper,' as she tried not to notice Reid's head turning in her direction. His eyes were shaded by sunglasses but she could *feel* his gaze on her body.

She suddenly wished she were wearing a bikini or even a one-piece. Something more flattering than her faded, long-sleeved rasher shirt. Sure, it was snug on her body, as were the Lycra bottoms that stopped just above her knee, but there was hardly any skin on show. Even her floppy, practical, Cancer-Council-approved hat felt suddenly daggy.

She might be being sun-sensible but she had about as much sex appeal as the bleached chunk of driftwood they'd passed higher up the beach.

She plonked herself quickly down beside Eddie, the sand cool and wet on the backs of her thighs as she turned her attention to Oscar's creation. *Instead* of the way sand clung to Reid's muscular calves.

'Wow, look at that moat,' she said.

'It was my idea,' Oscar said, puffing out his chest. 'I saw one in a book that Raymond brought to school.'

'How about we fill the buckets up with water and flood it?' Reid suggested.

Oscar's face came alive. 'Oh, yeah!' He grabbed a bucket. 'C'mon, Reid.'

He headed for the water's edge without a backward glance, Reid hot on his heels. Trinity's heart melted as they ran back and forth for what seemed an age, dumping their loads of water into the moat before heading back to the water's edge again.

The mother in her lapped it up. Lapping up the happiness of her son as he played without a care as if he'd never spent one hundred and eighty days in the NICU. The *woman* in her lapped it up too. Lapped up a bare-chested Reid, jogging and bending and twisting and turning, wet boardies clinging to powerful thighs.

And it wasn't just her. Other women checked him out too.

But they didn't just look. They *flirted*. Smiled at him and said, 'Hi,' as they walked past swinging their hips and wiggling their bare butts totally exposed in their teeny-tiny thongs.

It made absolutely no sense to be peeved about it. She was *not* with Reid. Never would be.

But she was peeved anyway.

Finally exhausted, Oscar and Reid collapsed on the sand near the castle, happy and laughing.

'Well,' Eddie announced, pushing to his feet. 'I'm going for a dip.'

Oscar suddenly sprang into a sitting position, staring after Eddie. 'Oh, could I go too, Mummy?'

'No, sweetie,' Trinity said. 'It's too deep and the current can be really strong. When you're older maybe.'

'I can take him,' Reid offered.

'Oh, yeah!' Oscar grinned at Reid before turning pleading eyes on his mother. 'Please, Mummy, can I go with Reid?'

Trinity looked out over the water. She was torn between the blatant begging and the thought of the current tearing Oscar from Reid's arms and sweeping him out to sea. 'Well...'

'Please.'

'I won't let him go. I promise.'

There was that low, gravelly voice again. She glanced at Reid, who'd taken off his sunglasses, the sincerity in his blue eyes as deep as the ocean. She believed him. Not only was he the strongest-looking man she'd ever met but he'd been nothing but protective of Oscar.

He'd asked her to trust him. Told her she could. *Proved* she could. Maybe it was time she showed him a little in return.

'Okay.' She glanced at her son. 'But not too deep,' she warned, raising her voice over Oscar's whooping.

Reid handed her his sunglasses as he stood. 'I won't go out higher than my waist.'

She stood too. 'And you'll hold onto him. Tight.'

'I will.' He held out his hand and Oscar took it.

Trinity grabbed Reid's arm as he stepped away. The skin was warm from the sun and the muscle beneath full and firm. He half turned, glancing at her hand before his gaze landed on her face. 'Thank you.'

He smiled and nodded then walked away with her son towards the ocean.

Reid and Oscar stayed in for close to an hour. He was so excited to be out in the deeper water, splashing around with the rest of their fellow ocean-goers, that Reid was determined to stay as long as Oscar wanted.

His mother needn't have worried about them being separated. For all his bravado, Oscar clung to him like a monkey, his breathing fast and excited as they'd waded in together.

Still, it didn't stop Trinity from pacing up and down the shoreline. She was easy to spot in bathers that would have been perfectly at home at Bondi a hundred years ago. Compared to the other scantily clad women she stuck out like a sore thumb, covered neck to knee, her hair stuffed up inside her big, floppy hat totally obscuring her face and eyes.

Even so, he could *feel* her gaze firmly fixed on him.

Well, *Oscar* anyway.

Reid, on the other hand, could hardly take his eyes off her. She might not have been exposing much skin but it was the first thing she'd worn that actually showed off her body and what she actually had going on under clothes that usually hung.

It was a novelty to be able to see she actually had a waist. And breasts that looked as if they'd fill a man's hand. He'd known they were there. Had felt them pressed to him, mashed up against him that day on her bed, but to see them... Or *glimpse* their outline anyway.

He'd spent an inordinate amount of time while playing with Oscar hoping she might get wet.

'Can we go out to Eddie?'

Pops was out in shoulder-deep water chatting to some other old guy and, while Reid was confident in his own abilities, he'd promised Trinity he wouldn't take Oscar out deep.

'Not this time, dude.'

Oscar took it on the chin as he did everything else. He was a good kid. Well behaved, not prone to sulking if he didn't get his way. Trinity had done an awesome job with him, considering their circumstances.

Not that he was any closer to knowing what

her true circumstances actually were. She might have relaxed around him but chatty she was not.

Oscar absently traced the outline of his eagle wings tat with one pruned finger. 'I like your tattoos,' he said.

Reid grinned. Oscar hadn't really mentioned them before—to him anyway—which was unusual. Most kids were agog. 'Thank you. Tattoos sometimes frighten kids but not you, huh?'

He shook his head. 'No. Mummy has a tattoo.'

Reid blinked. *Oh, does she now?* He glanced at her staring at them from the shoreline in her neck-to-knee gear. He really, *really* wished he hadn't known that. He was going to be thinking about it way more than was good for his sanity.

Already questions about where and what rose in his throat. But he was *not* going to pump her kid for information that was none of his damn business.

Oscar shivered and goose bumps broke out on his arms. Reid was pleased for the distraction. 'Cold, little dude?'

'No.'

Reid gave a half-laugh. He was on the cool side himself now but, on closer inspection, Oscar's lips were a nice shade of purple-blue and he was pretty sure Trinity would bundle him straight out if she were here. Because that was what a responsible parent did.

He'd never given a lot of thought to being a parent. A *father*. He'd assumed he would be one day but, at thirty-four, maybe he'd missed that boat?

Oscar's teeth started to chatter.

'Your teeth are chattering.'

'They're j…just exci…excited.'

Reid laughed again. *Excited teeth. Kids!*

'Yeah, I don't think your mum is going to buy that, dude, and she'll have my—' He cut himself off before he said *ass on a platter*. 'I'll be off her Christmas card list.'

Oscar nodded, resigned. 'Yeah. She always worries I might catch a bug and have to go to hospital.'

It was a natural thing for mothers to worry about, even though Reid knew no one caught a bug *just* from being cold. But there was a gravity to Oscar's words that told him it was a legitimate fear of Trinity's.

That Oscar had been in hospital before.

He opened his mouth to press for more then shut it again. He wasn't going to ask about that any more than he was going to ask about Trinity's

tattoo. He should just man up and do it himself—
the hospital thing, not the tattoo thing—instead
of waiting for her to open up to him.

Maybe he would ask her. In a few weeks.

In the meantime, he didn't want to start on the
wrong foot by handing over a hypothermic child.
He motioned to his grandfather to let him know
they were heading back. 'Okay, let's go in.'

Oscar sighed and put his head down on Reid's
shoulder. It fitted perfectly. Reid's heart gave a
strange little kick and the feeling of restlessness
that had dogged him since coming back to stay
with Pops stilled. After a moment's hesitation, he
placed his chin on top of the snowy-blond head
and strode out of the ocean with him.

'Mummy,' Oscar said as Reid placed him down
in ankle-deep water and he ran the rest of the
way, flinging his arms around Trinity's legs. 'Did
you see me?'

'I did, darling,' she said, smiling down at him,
obviously uncaring that Oscar was soaking wet.

She was, unfortunately, still depressingly dry.
Although now apparently the owner of a tattoo,
which only made her more fascinating. Not to

mention the fact he could see her nipples were erect through the cling of her rasher shirt.

He dragged his gaze off them, grabbed for his sunglasses, which dangled from her fingertips, and crammed them on his face. Now he could stare at them with impunity.

And he did. Friend zone or not.

No matter how much he castigated himself for acting like a horny teenager, he didn't seem to be able to stop.

'Goodness,' she said. 'You're freezing. Let's get you changed.'

There wasn't any reproach in her voice but, judging by her speed back to their belongings, she wanted Oscar dressed and warmed even though a few minutes in the sun would achieve the same thing.

By the time Reid had reached their little square of sand Oscar's rasher top was off and she was throwing a towel around his shoulders, rubbing his arms briskly.

'Reid,' Oscar said as he drew level. Trinity had turned and was searching through her bag behind her. 'You want to get warm with me?'

Oscar opened the towel, a cheeky grin on his face, exposing his puny little chest before Trinity turned back and pulled it around him and started rubbing again.

But not before Reid had seen what he'd seen. A long, pale scar running straight up the middle of Oscar's chest. An open-heart-surgery scar. And a couple of small round scars between his ribs on both sides. Chest drain insertion sites.

What the hell?

She always worries I might catch a bug and have to go to hospital.

Reid didn't doubt it. The sternotomy scar had confirmed his suspicion that Oscar had been in hospital before. *More than once* if those scars were what he thought they were.

So, Oscar had some kind of heart condition? It explained him being on the small side. Was this a chronic thing with chronic issues or was it something that had been dealt with and was in the past?

He didn't know but he wanted to and she could bet her ass he was *definitely* asking about it. No maybes. No in a few weeks.

Tonight.

A few hours later Trinity sat in the dark, on the love seat, appreciating the stars and the sounds of the night. The trilling of insects, the occasional distant sounds of a car and the muffled murmur of a television. They floated to her on the warm air along with the squeak of the hinges and she sighed contently.

It was moments like this that everything felt surreal. As if she were going to wake up tomorrow and find it was all a dream. She'd never imagined herself sitting idly on an old-fashioned swing, staring out over a beautiful back yard with absolutely nothing to do or worry about.

She hadn't been idle in five years and there'd always been *something* to worry about.

But here she was and she had Reid to thank for it. She was so damn grateful to him it filled up every cell and all the spaces in between. If she lived to be a million years old she'd never be able to repay him for what he'd done for her and Oscar.

Never.

The sound of dishes clanking together drifted to her from next door and the feeling that she should be doing something reared its head. But there wasn't anything. They'd had an early tea of fish and chips, then Oscar had gone for his first ever sleepover at Raymond's house.

Celia had rung as they'd been waiting for their food to be cooked and Oscar was so excited she hadn't been able to say no. Letting out the apron strings was a work in progress and she was taking baby steps every day. This had felt more like a giant leap but Reid had nodded almost imperceptibly and urged her with her eyes to take it and she had.

It was a *big deal* though. For her. There'd been very few nights in five years they'd spent apart. Even during his long hospital stays she'd slept most nights by his crib on lumpy, uncomfortable recliners.

She'd been allocated a small unit at the accommodation block for parents with children who had long-term illnesses but she'd rarely spent a night there. And even when she had succumbed to the nurse's urgings to get a decent sleep for a change, she'd usually ended back at his crib-side a couple of times during the night to express milk or just sit with him.

They'd sure come a long way since those early days. Oscar had gone from lengthy hospital stays to having sleepovers with friends, which was everything Trinity had ever wanted for him so she was going to have to get used to it. Hopefully, when they had their own place, Raymond could come and stay with them.

The sound of the sliding door opening interrupted her reverie. Right on cue, the hair at her nape prickled. 'Hey.'

The low rumble washed over her as the prickle headed south, beading her nipples and scattering goose bumps across her belly. 'Hey.'

'Beer?'

A bottle nudged her upper arm and she took it. 'Thanks.'

She cradled it in her lap, absently running her fingers up and down the frosty surface as he sat on the other end of the love seat, his right leg tucked up under him.

He didn't say anything for a while, just sipped his beer and stared out over the back yard. It was nice to sit in companionable silence, even if her body was excruciatingly aware of him. The bunch of his quad as he idly rocked the chair, the way his lips pressed against the neck of his beer and the movement of his throat as he tipped his head back and drank.

'I noticed Oscar's sternotomy scar on the beach today.'

CHAPTER TWELVE

TRINITY BLINKED AND her heart skipped a beat as she stared at him. Nothing like throwing a hand grenade to ruin the ambience. 'Oh.'

She'd seen it so often she didn't really see it at all any more. Except when he was in hospital battling lung infections and the scar stuck out horrifyingly white as he struggled for breath.

'I assume he had some congenital heart condition?'

Trinity hesitated. 'Yes.' She took a swallow of the beer and fixed her gaze on the distant stars.

'I hope you know you can talk to me, Trinity.'

His voice was soft and sincere. Calm. As if he were talking to a frightened animal that might scarper at any moment. She wasn't frightened though. Not of telling Reid. She was just so used to *not* telling people, actually opening up about it was surprisingly difficult.

Of course, there were plenty of people who knew about Oscar's condition—most of them medical. Also a handful of strangers—parents of sick kids—she'd met over the years whenever Oscar had been an inpatient. The bond formed with someone who was living the same nightmare encouraged those kinds of confidences.

And the school too, of course.

But she didn't tend to talk about it as a general rule. Especially not to people she didn't know well. She hadn't wanted it to draw attention to Oscar as being different or remarkable. Flying under the radar was what she'd perfected.

A bit of that old tension slid into her bones as she contemplated opening up. She took a deep breath. 'He had Tetralogy of Fallot.'

There was a pause. 'I see.' She could feel his gaze lasering into her profile. 'TOFs are pretty routine cardiac repairs these days. Lots of great paediatric cardiac surgeons out there. Were there complications?'

The tension oozed from Trinity's bones at his matter-of-fact reply. Reid probably knew more about TOF than she did and not having to explain that the condition consisted of four different cardiac defects and what that meant physiologically was a relief. It still didn't stop the rise of hysterical laughter spilling from her throat. TOF repairs were routine enough but Oscar's case had been somewhat complicated.

'You could say that.'

'Yeah. I thought that might be the case. Why don't you start at the beginning?'

Trinity had a choice now. To gloss over the details and move on. Or open up. Reid had taken her and Oscar in, given them a roof and an income and hadn't pried into the circumstances of her life and she was surprised to find she *wanted* to tell him.

Maybe it was because he'd never pushed. Maybe it was his medical knowledge. Maybe it was their fledgling friendship.

Or maybe it was the funny sensation in the centre of her chest today as she'd watched him hold Oscar in the ocean.

Whatever. She *wanted* to tell him.

'Oscar was born at twenty-six weeks.'

Reid whistled. 'Okay. That explains his size.'

'Yes.'

'Was the TOF diagnosed via ultrasound prenatally?'

Trinity shook her head, the rush of guilt she always felt about her lack of prenatal care as keen as ever.

'No. I…didn't know I was pregnant until I was about sixteen weeks and then…' God. Then she hadn't known what to do. 'I was nineteen. I was living on the streets. I didn't really know what to do except I knew I had to get my act together because I did *not* want that kind of life for Oscar.'

'Do you mind me asking why you were on the streets?'

Trinity hesitated. This conversation wasn't about her but she supposed it was only natural that it would go there. She was surprised to find she wanted to tell him about that as well.

'A dysfunctional home life. Parents caught in an intergenerational welfare cycle who spent most of their money on things like booze and cigarettes and the pokies and spent the rest of their time fighting and wrecking whatever hovel we were in at the time. Lots of police call-outs. Then they'd break up and there'd be a whole conga line of new boyfriends or girlfriends before they got back together again. School was a godsend but my parents usually felt their hangover needs were greater than my scholastic ones so I missed more school than I attended.'

Trinity stopped, aware she was talking too fast as she plucked the events of her youth out of her brain from the macabre carousel going around and around. She took another sip of her beer, staring at the stars. It was easier to tell when she wasn't looking at him.

Especially the next bit.

'And then when I was seventeen my mum's latest boyfriend decided he wanted to try a threesome. With her. And me. She was okay with that...but I wasn't.'

Trinity was pleased for the cover of night as her face blazed. That conversation still made her cringe to this day. The way he'd leered at her as if she were the cherry on his pie still made her skin crawl. Reid didn't say anything, for which she was grateful. He just sat and listened, his foot rocking the chair.

'So I walked away. Actually I ran away and never went back. I hooked up with Brian, a guy I knew from having met him in courts and cop stations on and off over the years because of our parents. He was a few years older than me and had had it worse. He'd been in and out of the foster system for years. He was living on the streets but he welcomed me with open arms, showed me the ropes.'

A tendril of the fear that had gripped her in

those first few days she'd been alone curled around her gut and Trinity paused for a moment.

Reid must have sensed it because he drew in air between his teeth and said, 'Tough life.'

It wasn't trite *or* judgemental, just a statement of fact.

'It's not for the faint-hearted,' Trinity admitted, finally looking at him. Their gazes locked. 'But it was more harmonious living on the streets with him than it had ever been under my parents' roof. There's a whole homeless community out there and I know it's screwed up but for the first time in my life I felt like people cared about me. That they actually gave a damn.'

He nodded and she felt as if he really understood. 'Is that where you learned to fight?'

Trinity laughed at the unexpected question. 'Yeah. One of the guys we knew was some kind of ex-black-ops dude. I learned enough from him to get by.'

He stroked his beard and the sound became a physical caress down her body. He took a swallow of his beer. 'So... Brian's Oscar's dad?'

'Yes.'

'Is he...around? Involved at all?'

'No. Bri died a couple of months after Oscar was born.'

'I'm sorry.'

His voice had deepened and the resonance of his sincerity was like a physical force. 'Don't be. He was stoned and apparently playing chicken with a train. I loved him but he always did have a bit of a death wish.'

The wince on Reid's face said it all. 'He was a pot-head?'

'Oh, yes.'

It hadn't bothered Trinity that Brian was high seventy-five per cent of the time. Not before she was pregnant. But after—it had mattered a lot.

'Have I shocked you?'

'No. Not at all.' He half turned on the chair to face her. 'I went off the rails a bit in my teens. Divorced parents, shipped between two warring parties, a string of new partners who all wanted to *be my friend*.' He waved his hand in the air dismissively to indicate the usual stuff. 'I was angry…ran away. Fell in with the wrong crowd. Got into some petty crime, was in trouble with the cops a bit. My parents disowned me. It was Pops actually who took me in, turned me around.'

Reid had been into petty crime? It wasn't that

hard *looking* at him to imagine him being on the wrong side of the law. He *looked* as if he belonged in an outlaw motorcycle gang. But *knowing* him was a different matter. The big, motorbike-riding, tat-covered, bearded man was the opposite of how he appeared.

'That was very good of Eddie.' Any extended family Trinity owned had all been cut from the same cloth as her parents.

None of them had wanted her either.

'I hadn't had much to do with him at that point. My father and he didn't get along very well but my grandmother had died a few years before and he needed somewhere to put his love and attention as much as I needed love and attention.'

Trinity nodded. 'That sounds like Bri and me.' He'd taken her under his wing as much for himself as for her.

'You were with him?' Reid asked gently. 'When he died?'

'No. We'd already split by then.'

'You'd split?'

She nodded. 'He wanted me to get an abortion. He didn't want to waste any of his precious pot money on a kid. It was him or the baby.'

'Ah. I see.'

'I went there,' she said, dropping her gaze to her beer bottle, picking at the label absently. 'To the clinic. That's where I found out how far along I was. They did an ultrasound. And, of course, at sixteen weeks I couldn't just get a pill and be done with it. But that was okay because I'd seen him on the screen, this little skeletal creature scuttling around, sucking his thumb and… I knew I couldn't do it.'

'They didn't pick up the TOF on that ultrasound?'

'No, it was mainly just for dates. I was supposed to go at nineteen weeks for a proper one but I was couch-surfing and trying to find a job and sort my life out and, frankly, scared out of my wits and I told myself I'd go later for another check-up, towards the end, but…'

'You went into premature labour.'

'Yes.'

'It's okay. They're often not picked up on ultrasound anyway.'

A block of unexpected emotion welled in her chest and lodged in her throat. 'It's not okay. I should have taken better care of myself. Of him. It was…irresponsible.'

'You weren't to know. There was nothing they could have done antenatally anyway.'

'*I* could have done something.'

He shrugged. 'Maybe knowing about it might have helped with forward planning but—'

'No,' she choked out, interrupting him, the beer label half shredded. 'I mean I could have prevented the TOF if I'd known about Oscar earlier.'

He frowned and shook his head very slowly, his gaze fixing on hers. 'Trinity…it's a congenital defect. It happened when Oscar's heart was forming. There's nothing you could have done about that.'

She shook her head. 'It was my fault.'

It was the one phrase she'd never dared speak out loud and now she had. If she'd hoped there'd be some kind of catharsis, some lightening of her burden, she was badly mistaken.

'I fell pregnant in winter,' she said, her voice husky, her heart heavy, her emotions sitting in a giant tangle in her gut. She returned her attention to the label. 'It's cold on the streets in winter. We'd been drinking cask red wine to help keep warm. I mean, I never drank much, nowhere near as much as others. Maybe a couple of glasses every night and I stopped when I found out I was pregnant…immediately. But I've Googled it.'

She shut her eyes. It was a hard thing to admit that a substance she'd put in her body had caused Oscar's condition. That she was responsible for his malformed heart.

'Trinity.'

His voice was low, vibrating with compassion. She sucked in a breath. 'They say drinking alcohol can affect the formation of the growing foetal heart and—'

'Trinity.'

She peeped at him through her fringe. He moved closer, the chair rocking a little. Sliding a finger under her chin, he raised it until she was looking him square in the eye. She shivered at the compassion warming his blue gaze.

Or maybe it was his touch.

'They don't know anything definitively.'

Trinity desperately wanted to believe that. 'But—'

'The foetal heart is pretty near formed by six weeks,' he interrupted again. 'TOF is not a common condition. A lot of women don't even know they're pregnant until then. You want to guess how many of them are blissfully drinking unawares during that time? There'd be a helluva lot more TOF if booze was the causal factor, don't you think?'

Trinity hadn't thought of it like that before. Of the bigger picture. Of the many women who'd drunk alcohol while pregnant with absolutely no ill effects on their babies. She'd just read it online and been instantly paralysed by guilt.

'I guess.'

'A risk factor is just that. It doesn't mean that's what caused Oscar's condition. They. Don't. Know.' He whispered the last three words, taking the time to emphasise each one, staring deep into her eyes, as if he was willing her to believe.

For the first time in five years she actually did.

She doubted the guilt over his condition would ever completely disappear. As a struggling single mother, Trinity had found that guilt lay around every corner. But Reid had given her perspective.

She swallowed. 'Okay.'

'Yeah?' He cocked an eyebrow.

Trinity gave a half-smile. 'Yeah.'

'Good.'

He smiled and released her chin. He didn't shift away though and she was hyperaware of her body's reaction to his nearness. Of his finger imprint under her chin, of the dark shadow of his beard and tats, of the way his T-shirt fell against his belly.

The long stretch of his thigh.

Every cell in her body seemed to be undergoing a chemical reaction. Melting down.

'So,' Reid said after a beat or two, turning back to face the night, 'he was born at twenty-six weeks with a TOF? I'm guessing that complicated things rather a lot.'

Trinity struggled to gather her wits and pick up the threads of what they'd been talking about before they'd become sidetracked by their own life stories.

'Ah...yes.' She took a sip of her beer to cool the heat of her body.

'What did he weigh?'

'Eight hundred and twenty grams.'

'*Oh.*' He glanced at her. 'Under a kilo.'

'Yes.' The fact she didn't have to tell him that premmie babies under a kilo had much poorer outcomes was a relief. 'Obviously he had tiny lungs, which weren't helped by the severe pulmonary stenosis from his condition. Worst the specialist had seen apparently,' she said, her tone derisive.

'Hell. He really had the odds stacked against him, didn't he?'

'Oh, yes,' she said with a self-deprecating smile. 'This is why I look old and haggard.'

He snorted. 'You don't look old and haggard.'

She blushed at his quick dismissal, his compliment rushing dangerously to her head. '*You* thought I was older than twenty-four,' she accused, keeping her voice light.

'I said you *acted* older.' He grinned at her. 'Different thing entirely.'

Trinity's breath hitched at his grin and the fact that she returned it. Why was he so damn easy to talk to?

'So how old was he when they did the repair?'

'He had a shunt initially as a stopgap measure until he grew big enough to have the surgery, but he was five months, two months corrected age, before he was big enough and well enough to have the full open-heart surgical repair. He was in the NICU for one hundred and eighty days.'

He whistled. 'That sounds incredibly stressful.'

'It was.' Trinity shuddered. How she'd got through it she had no idea. 'There were so many hairy moments. It seems he takes after his father in the dicing-with-death department.'

'So what did you do while he was in the NICU all that time?'

She blinked. 'Nothing. I stayed with him. I *couldn't* leave him.' Her gaze met his; she needed him to understand. 'Plus it was a solution to my housing problem. They have units at the hospital for long-term families. They weren't anything flash but it was like a palace compared to what I was used to. They charged a nominal rent so I was able to save some of my government money for use when he was finally discharged.'

He gave an incredulous half-laugh. 'Did *no one* guess you'd come from the streets?'

'Nope.' She shook her head. 'I became really good at pretence and flying under the radar. I used my parents' address and told them I still lived at home with my mum, who was house bound with crippling agoraphobia. They knew I wasn't with Oscar's dad any more but I was there and engaged in Oscar's care. I was sane and stable. I didn't cause waves or rock any boats. I...became part of the furniture, I guess. They *knew* me. Well, they knew the kind of person I was anyway. That I was a good mother and that Oscar would be in good hands and that's what mattered.'

'But…' he angled himself in the swing to face her again '…you could have talked to social services. They would have hooked you up with all kinds of support. You could have put down for public housing.'

Trinity shook her head. 'The wait list is *years*.'

'But you'd have been fast-tracked if they'd known your situation.'

She was stupidly touched by his earnestness. 'And in the meantime the authorities know I'm not able to provide for my son and they take him off me?' She shook her head. 'If they'd found out I'd been homeless and I had no idea where I was going to live if Oscar was ever well enough to go home, I'd have never seen him again. And I wasn't risking that.'

The one thing Trinity and people like her, who grew up in the kinds of places she had and who'd lived on the streets, had been conditioned to mistrust, was social services. It might have been wrong but it was deep-seated and compelling.

Even the thought of it now was enough to make her blood run cold.

Oscar was her son. She'd sat and watched too

often as he'd fought to survive, to breathe, to live. There wasn't any system she wouldn't have fought to keep them together.

CHAPTER THIRTEEN

'So...' HE STARED into her eyes, confusion in his own. 'Where *did* you go? Have you been homeless for five years?'

'No.' Trinity shook her head vehemently. It was important that Reid knew she hadn't been irresponsible with her son's welfare. 'I told you, that's only been a few times.'

'Okay.' He held up his hands in surrender. 'I believe you.'

'Initially I was able to rent a room in a share house. I got a job as a cleaner at a small hotel. The boss allowed me to bring Oscar to work. I strapped him to my chest and went with him from room to room. But then Oscar caught a bug and it knocked him flat. This time he ended up in Paediatric Intensive Care for two weeks. I lost my job. And the accommodation.'

'So. He's had ongoing problems?'

'Multiple readmissions with respiratory infections. Multiple ventilations. Many, many weeks and months in hospital. In fact he's spent more of his life in hospital than out of it.'

'I'm assuming that meant a lot of lost jobs and accommodation.'

'Yes.' Trinity grimaced. 'We got by though. I always found work again and another place to live. But…it was stressful. Nowhere near as stressful as seeing your kid hooked up to monitors and machines, struggling to breathe though.'

He nodded and she could see in his eyes that he knew what it was like to witness someone in respiratory distress.

'You wouldn't know it now,' he said. 'I mean, he's a little pale and a bit on the skinny side but he seems healthy. He's bright and alert and has oodles of energy.'

Trinity smiled. 'It's been six months since his last admission at the beginning of winter. The specialists told me he should improve as he grew and his lungs got bigger and I'm starting to hope that he really *is* over the worst of it. Knock on wood.'

She looked around for some wood but in the wrought-iron love seat there was nothing. She wasn't superstitious but she'd learned not to tempt any kind of fate where Oscar's health was concerned. Reid smiled and dipped his head towards her for Trinity to knock.

She stared at the long glossy hair for a few moments. A patch of dull gleamed where it caught the muted starlight. The urge to tunnel her fingers into it, to sift through it, almost overrode her need to pander to superstition. Not trusting herself, she gave a quick knock, her knuckles protesting as they met unyielding skin and bone.

'*Ow.*' She gave a half-laugh as she withdrew her hand, rubbing the bony knobs absently. 'I think it's made of rock, not wood.'

He lifted his head and grinned at her. 'Are you accusing me of being hard-headed, Ms Walker?'

Trinity's breath hitched at the lightness in his gaze, at the tease. Almost as if he was...flirting. The knowledge whispered against her nipples and trembled through her thighs.

'Well,' she said, smiling at him, trying to keep it friendly and not flirty, which was what they'd agreed to, 'your head did almost break my knuckles.'

He threw his head back and laughed, big and full and strong, and her heart fluttered a wild tango as the deep, rich sound resonated through every cell of her being. Her gaze fell helplessly to the bare stretch of his neck, to the line where his beard ended and his throat began. To the thick thud of the pulse bounding just within touching distance.

Licking distance.

The laughter cut out and he lowered his chin until his eyes met hers again. 'I've been called worse. Including *soft*-headed.'

Trinity smiled at his self-deprecation. 'Well, I don't know about that but definitely soft-hearted.'

His low dismissive snort oozed all over her, her breath stuttering to a halt as his gaze strayed, zeroing in on her mouth. He stared at it—hard. As if he was mapping its contours, deciding just how he was going to kiss it.

Her pulse fluttered madly at her pulse points.

There wasn't much distance separating them, he could lean in and his lips would be on hers in a heartbeat and for a crazy moment she thought he was actually going to do it. He made a slight, almost imperceptible, move towards her. Less than a move, really, more a disruption of the air currents.

But then it was gone, in the blink of an eye, leaving nothing but her madly pounding heart.

'Okay,' he muttered, swivelling his eyes forward again, shaking his head. 'I think I should *definitely* leave now.'

It wasn't a question. It was a statement. A purely rhetorical one that required none of her input. He drained his drink. 'Thank you,' he said, not looking at her, staring out into the night instead. 'For telling me about your stuff. I know it's not something you usually talk about and I appreciate that you shared it with me. I'm really sorry that you've had to go through all you've had to go through. I'm sorry that life is so unfair to so many while it's abundantly good to others.'

Before she had a chance to answer, the love seat was swinging crazily and he was gone, passing in front of her like a shadow. Trinity blinked as the door slid and clicked shut behind her.

Soft-hearted indeed.

Five hours later, Trinity was still wide awake staring at the ceiling. She'd like to pretend that it was because Oscar wasn't snuggled in bed with her or that she was fretting about how he was getting on at Raymond's, but that would be a lie.

She was lying awake thinking about *that* moment with Reid. The one where he'd almost kissed her. If that was what it had been. If it hadn't been a trick of the dark. If her fevered body hadn't just…imagined it.

But it was circling around and around in her head, refusing to leave.

He'd looked at her mouth as if he'd wanted to devour it. As if he'd wanted to *own* it. And the way he'd lectured himself about needing to go inside? As if he was trying to convince *himself.* *Compel* himself.

Because why?

Because he might be too tempted to kiss her if he stayed?

For so long now she'd been denying that Reid was really attracted to her. Telling herself that the great dry-humping incident had been mostly one-sided and he'd just reacted as any red-blooded man would. That it was only her who thought about kissing him way more than was good for her. Who dreamed erotic dreams. Who woke with her body on fire and an ache between her legs.

It seemed ludicrous that he could reciprocate such desires. He was a well-to-do, successful, self-assured guy. He had a home, a job, he had family and every kind of creature comfort. He wasn't hard up for *anything.*

She'd bet he wasn't hard up for women either.

Just because she'd never seen a woman and he spent all his time either at work or home with Eddie, Oscar and her, didn't mean there wasn't one.

Why would he lust after some chick who came with a sickly kid and more baggage than an airport who he'd plucked off the street?

Trinity's fist curled into the sheet and she rolled on her side, a frustrated growl gurgling in the back of her throat. She stuffed her hands between her legs, pressing hard to ease the ache that was slowly becoming a roar.

She couldn't deny how much she wanted him. How this feeling had grown from an initial flare of attraction to a full-blown obsession. Was it possible that he could actually want her too?

The man did funny things to her heart, things she *didn't understand* and didn't want to examine too closely. But what he did to her body she *did* understand.

Desire and passion had been dormant in her for so long but they were *roaring* to life with a potency that was blinding. Trinity tried to convince herself it was because it had been an age since she'd felt them but deep down she knew it was because of the man who'd roused them.

She rolled onto her back, her body burning as she stared at the ceiling. If she had any kind of courage she'd slip into bed with him and find out once and for all whether that look in his eyes tonight had been real or imagined.

Why not? Oscar wasn't home and Eddie, all the way downstairs, would never hear them. Her heart beat so frantically at the illicit thought, it practically exploded out of her chest.

But…she couldn't. *She was no seductress.* She lacked the guts. *And* the finesse.

Something bumped in the hallway and her heart stopped with one loud definitive bang. Her breath cut off with a strangled gargle high in her throat. Her limbs froze.

Reid?

Her eyes darted to the door. Was he coming *to her*? Had he been lying awake too, burning with desire, wishing he'd kissed her?

Was *he* coming to seduce *her*?

Trinity shut her eyes and wished like hell he was. It was selfish and indulgent and very possibly *crazy* but she didn't care.

Her ears strained for the slightest noise. Anything that indicated it *might* be him. But there were no footsteps. She couldn't hear her name being called. Her door didn't open.

Nothing.

Then she heard it again, followed by a loud meow outside her door. Her breath burst from starving lungs, her heart kicked in, belting along like a runaway train, her limbs jerked back into use as she rolled off the bed and opened the door for Ginger, who had taken to joining them in the middle of the night, much to Oscar's delight.

The cat strutted in and Trinity's gaze followed the high, proud flick of its tail as it leapt onto the bed. She looked down the end of the hallway where Reid's door stood open. He never slept with it shut because he wanted to be able to hear his grandfather if he called out in the middle of the night.

But now it just sat there open. Taunting her. Nothing but night shadows on the other side, beckoning her to the dark side. She willed him to appear in the doorway but of course he didn't.

He wasn't coming for her.

Of course he wasn't coming for her.

If she wanted to have a night of passion with Reid then she was going to have to make the first move because he was too honourable to do so himself. He'd told her he would never take advantage of the situation and she'd learned enough about him these past weeks to know that he wouldn't break that promise, no matter how much he might have wanted to kiss her earlier.

Trinity stared at the door, her heart racing, torn between the needs of her body and the dictates of her head. It had been five years—*longer*—since she'd been with a man. Given herself up to sexual pleasure. Well, apart from a spot of dry humping with Reid.

She flushed at the memory even as her body tingled from top to toe. One thing she knew for sure: she was never going to be able to sleep like this and she didn't want to lie in bed tossing and turning all night, aware of the ache between her legs and him just down the hallway.

Not even a session of self-love to take the edge off appealed. Her body burned for one person only. Her fingers just weren't going to cut it.

She sighed. Lying horizontal in a bed was not going to take her mind off what her body craved. If anything it was going to keep reminding her of what she couldn't have. She needed a distraction. So, she was going to take her book—a hard-core science-fiction tome—go downstairs, make a cup of tea and read it in the living room until she fell asleep.

Problem solved.

The moon had risen in the hours Trinity had lain in bed and milky moonlight flooded into the kitchen through the large bay window. It spilled over the central bench and the floor, turning the already white kitchen candescent. She stood at the sink, glass of water in hand as she waited for the jug to boil, staring out of the window, soaking up the moonbeams.

It was so beautiful she had a mad urge to strip off her clothes and run around in it.

Yeah, just what Reid needed. *Not.* A crazy, pagan woman running around his back yard in the nuddy. She really had to do something about her horniness or she'd be howling at the moon next.

Another thump behind her dragged her gaze from the window. Damn cat.

Except it wasn't the cat.

It was Reid. In nothing but boxer shorts. The sexy kind that clung to *everything*. As if her hormone-crazed brain needed any more stimulus.

He was standing beyond the line of moonlight

but she could still make out the dark outline of his tats and his beard. Not to mention his shoulders, hips and quads.

The contours of his boxers too.

Trinity clenched the sink behind her. And her legs together as everything inside her dropped about a foot. Her pulse tripped as if she'd taken a little something other than the desperation of five years of celibacy.

Like cocaine.

'Reid?' Her voice was almost a squeak and she cleared it.

'Oh…sorry.' The apology rumbled out. 'I couldn't sleep.'

'Me either,' she said, her voice several octaves lower now, more husky than squeaky.

His eyes were hooded in shadow but she could *feel* his gaze eating her up. She was in her tatty old T-shirt that was too big for her and had a hole in the sleeve. It was about as sexy as a sack.

'I was just coming to get a drink.'

The way he said it left Trinity in no doubt that he hadn't been heading to the kitchen for a cup of tea. More like beer.

'You want one?' he asked as he strode out of the shadows into the full blaze of moonlight. It bathed his body to perfection, delineating every dip, line and contour. Every tattoo. Every muscle group.

Trinity pushed through a temporary circuit failure in her brain. 'No... I'm just making tea.'

He didn't head for the fridge but for the high cupboards, reaching up effortlessly for something and placing it on the central bench.

A bottle of Jack. The big guns.

He opened the dishwasher that had finished its cycle hours ago and pulled out a glass that sparkled with diamond clarity in the alabaster light and *tinked* as it was placed on the bench top. He unscrewed, poured a slug into the glass, then threw his head back and downed it in one hit.

He didn't even wince.

'You sure you don't want one?'

Trinity shook her head, crossing to the bench where the boiled jug was waiting to be poured. She slid the glass of water onto the counter top and tipped hot water into the waiting mug, teabag already in situ.

'You going to read?' he asked, tipping his chin at her book that also sat on the bench top.

'Yes.'

A muscle worked in his jaw as he glanced from

her to the book then back to her. His knuckles whitened where they gripped the edge of the bench and he looked as if he was about to say something else but he didn't, just poured himself another drink.

She crossed to the fridge as he downed that one too. She grabbed the milk and poured some into her cup, conscious of his gaze on her. It cranked every muscle in her body to attention.

'Reading helps put me to sleep when my mind is going round and round,' she said, needing to fill up the brooding silence in case she took leave of her senses and got grabby.

'Worried about Oscar?'

'A little.' Although God knew that was *not* what was keeping her awake.

'Reading doesn't help me sleep,' he said, his voice gruff.

'You've tried?'

'Army psychologist recommended it for post-nightmare management.'

Trinity slid her mug on the bench. She took a step closer. 'You have nightmares?' She supposed he must have seen some terrible things while in the military.

'Not a lot,' he dismissed, his tone terse, clearly not wanting to elaborate.

Trinity backed off. 'And the Scotch helps?'

'Usually.' He poured himself a third.

'Not tonight?'

'Apparently.' He swirled the liquid in the glass, watching it intently.

'So...' She turned sideways, her hip resting against the counter. 'Were nightmares keeping you up tonight?'

A short sharp laugh escaped his lips. 'Not nightmares.' He shook his head, still staring into his drink. 'Dreams.'

He glanced at her then, his gaze lasering into hers. 'You know the type?'

The timbre of his breathing roughened, becoming a tangible force. Caressing right between her legs. The caress became an ache, which morphed into a screaming demand.

The man had also been having sex dreams. She swallowed. 'Yes,' she said, her voice not much more than a husky whisper.

'God, Trinity,' he muttered, throwing the last drink down and hauling her close. 'I'm drowning here.'

Reid was insensible with need as his mouth

took hers. He'd come to the kitchen for a drink or two to obliterate the nagging desire that constantly pulled at him, to stop himself from knocking on her door, to *do the right thing.*

Only to find temptation waiting for him in the moonlight in a baggy T-shirt, her hair long and loose.

She moaned against his mouth as his hands grabbed the backs of her thighs and hauled her up, settling her on the bench with her legs wide apart. Moving on autopilot, he stepped between them, his body knowing exactly where it needed to be. His crotch aligned perfectly with the heat at the juncture of her thighs as her ankles locked tight around his back telling him he was exactly where she needed him too.

God, yes, this. This was what he'd been craving.

Trinity.

His hands slid up her thighs under the loose T-shirt, around to her ass then up her back, rucking the shirt up as he went, exposing more and more of her to his view. His nostrils filled with the scent of her, her soap and shampoo and the earthier scent of her arousal. His ears reverberated with the pounding of his pulse and the frantic nonsensical noises coming from the back of her throat.

His hands moved around to cup her bare breasts and she cried out, breaking off their kiss, her head falling back as he brushed his thumbs over her nipples. He took her hands from his waist and laid them palm down on the counter top, sliding them back behind her, forcing her torso into a slight recline, presenting her breasts to him.

'Don't move,' he whispered, staring at them. Not too big, not too small, the rosy tips almost alabaster in the moon's glow.

He ducked to nuzzle one, swirling his tongue around it, knowing the whiskers of his beard would also be prickling against the sensitive flesh. She gasped and he repeated the process on the other side before sucking it deep into the hot cavern of his mouth.

She moaned and arched her back and it went straight to Reid's groin. *'Reid.'*

He taunted it, stretching it with his teeth and tongue as far as it would go before it slipped from his mouth. 'They're perfect,' he muttered. 'You're perfect,' before seeking the other one.

Reid couldn't get enough. Of her nipples. Or the way she arched into his mouth, her hair almost brushing against the bench top every time, or the increasingly desperate noises Trinity made at the back of her throat.

Knowing that he was getting her so damn hot was intoxicating.

He was so lost in the pleasure of it he didn't realised she'd manoeuvred herself more upright until her fingers breached the band of his underwear. They slid onto the taut flesh of his erection, wrapping around him, squeezing and sliding up and down.

He groaned, his mouth leaving her nipples to press his forehead against hers. *'God, yes.'*

He shut his eyes as pleasure rolled through him from his thighs to his buttocks. To the sling of muscles deep inside his pelvis to his abdominals. It moved in one long, luxurious undulation that weakened his knees as well as his resistance. The urge to find release between her thighs, slake his unruly desire for her, ran hot and insistent through his veins.

And then an almighty smash stopped them in their tracks.

His brain still fogged, Reid glanced over to find Ginger, sitting on the bench where Trinity's glass of water had been seconds before.

'*Miaow.*'

His heart thundered in his chest as he glanced at Trinity like a siren in the moonlight, her shirt rucked up, her chest rising and falling fast, beard burn marking her breasts and throat, her eyes glazed…

What the *hell* was he doing? What about being platonic? And friendship?

What about not crossing that line?

'God…' He shoved a hand through his hair, sucking in air, trying to regulate his breathing. 'We shouldn't be doing this.'

He yanked her shirt down, stuffed his erection back in his pants and took a step back. Then another, holding his hands up and away from his body. And hers. Not worried about broken glass. Just their predicament.

She stared at him, her tongue darting out to wet her lips. 'Right.' Although she didn't sound convinced.

'We agreed to be platonic.'

'Yes.' She nodded. 'But.'

The but didn't need anything added to it. He knew what it meant. *But look at us anyway,* not *being platonic.*

God, he was too keyed up for this. Too horny. Too close to the edge.

'Do you think we can talk about it in the morning?'

Maybe in the morning he wouldn't feel so much like pushing her down on the cold stone bench top and burying his head between her legs until she screamed his name. He was one yank of his underwear from penetration and he needed some distance.

'Okay.' She glanced at the smashed glass.

'I'll take care of it,' he assured her hastily.

She looked at him for long moments, the confusion on her face rather unhelpfully spotlighted by the moon, before finally swinging her legs around the other side of the bench, away from the broken glass, and sliding off. He watched her until she disappeared into the shadows.

If he'd thought her leaving would make him feel better, he was sadly mistaken.

CHAPTER FOURTEEN

THEY DIDN'T TALK about it the next morning, or the next day or the next, or the next. And now it was Thursday and Trinity was sitting waiting for Eddie's physio appointment to finish, being ignored by Reid, who did not have a patient but was squirrelled away in his office anyway. She could see him through the window that faced the central rehab area.

Trinity had tried to talk to Reid about it on Sunday but he'd dismissed her attempts irritably and had pretty much been irritable ever since.

With her anyway.

He was obviously regretting his slip in judgement big time. Because he'd stepped over the line he'd told her he wasn't going to step over again and Reid was a man of his word. But that could have easily been addressed on Sunday.

So it had to be more.

Like maybe he just didn't fancy her. Sure, he was *attracted* to her but was it because of *her* or because she was a woman and he was a man and they were in close proximity?

A person didn't have to like another person to have sex with them, after all. Her parents were a classic example of that.

She'd thought his talk about dreams had referred to her but maybe he'd been dreaming about someone else and she'd just been a convenient body to slake his thirst and then the glass had smashed and he'd suddenly realised *who* he was with.

The thought hurt. More than it should have. But she should have known that a guy like Reid couldn't possibly be into a woman like her.

'Hey, Trinity. Now aren't you a sight for sore eyes.'

She glanced up from her magazine to find Chase beaming down at her. His smile was a balm to her ravaged ego and she beamed right back.

At least someone was into her.

'Hey,' she said as he lowered himself into the hard plastic chair beside her, his high-tech prosthetic leg almost completely bared in his workout shorts. 'You're here for your session?'

'Nah, I only came to flirt with you. But don't

tell Reid. He can be a grumpy bastard when he wants to be.'

Trinity laughed. *Wasn't that the truth?* She caught a movement in her peripheral vision and glanced over. Reid was standing in his doorway, looking at her and Chase, his lips pursed, his brow furrowed, disapproval pouring off him in waves.

He didn't look like any kind of doctor in his jeans and dark T-shirt, his arm tats on full display. Not even the stethoscope slung casually around his neck helped. He just looked like a... lumberjack with a stethoscope.

Which was seriously freaking hot. *Damn him.*

'Shouldn't you be hitting the machines?' Reid said, folding his arms.

'All in good time.' Chase winked at her and Trinity stifled another laugh.

Reid stiffened. 'We have three people arriving in half an hour. If you don't get on now you'll miss out.'

He turned and stalked back into his room. Chase whistled. 'Who put a bug up his ass?'

'I have no idea.'

Except she did. And it couldn't go on. She made a mental note to contact some local real-estate agents this week. Might as well get the ball rolling.

'Well—' Chase stood '—I'd better get on before he gives me a yellow card.'

He smiled at Trinity, not looking remotely concerned about any consequences Reid might dish out. She glanced in the direction of Reid's office, catching him looking at her, before he returned his attention to his computer.

Well, screw him.

He couldn't reject her and then be annoyed that some other guy was interested. She left the magazine on the chair beside her and wandered over to Chase, who was starting his warm up.

She could feel the burn of Reid's gaze in the centre of her back as she sat on the floor beside Chase and chatted. In fact she relished it. It was utterly childish but it felt damn good.

Chase wasn't fooled though. 'So I'm guessing you're over here with me to make Reid jealous. Am I right?'

Trinity blinked at his directness. But Chase didn't seem perturbed by the prospect. 'Jealous? No.' *Absolutely not.* 'To piss him off, yes.'

Chase laughed a wicked laugh. 'That works for me.'

* * *

Trinity was in the kitchen making a banana cake when Reid came home. She tensed as she glanced at the clock—ten past two. His footsteps diverted to the living room and she heard the rumble of two male voices for a couple of minutes.

Then he appeared in the kitchen.

He hesitated for a moment when he spotted her at the bench before nodding and crossing to the fridge. He pulled out a beer, twisted the top and tossed it into the sink from where he stood.

It landed with a clink.

He tipped his head back and took several long swallows. It took all Trinity's willpower to keep her eyes on the job at hand and not feast her gaze on his neck.

'You do know Chase flirts with every woman with a pulse, right?'

The sentence came from out of the blue. She'd been in a good mood since returning from Allura. But Reid seemed hell-bent on ruining that too.

'Gee thanks,' she said, her voice dripping with sarcasm as a spike of temper infected her bloodstream. 'You sure know how to make a girl feel *real* special.'

'Oh, for—' He bit off whatever expletive he'd been about to utter. 'I just meant you should be careful. The guy wouldn't know monogamy if it bit him on the ass.'

'Who says I'm after monogamy?'

He blinked, clearly taken aback. *Good.* A slightly crazed sensation pushed at the inside of her skull as an urge to let fly took hold. She'd learned not to argue over the years. Not to rock the boat. To grind her teeth and quietly submit.

But, he was really starting to annoy her now.

'I would have thought being a single mum and having to think about Oscar—'

'*Don't* bring Oscar into this.'

'I'm just saying,' Reid pushed, obviously not going to let it drop. 'He's not daddy material.'

'I'm not going to marry the man,' Trinity said, letting the spoon fall to the bench with a loud clatter as she crossed to the pantry and opened the doors.

She searched the shelves for vanilla. She knew it was in here because Reid used it to make French toast on the weekends.

God, she'd never be able to eat French toast again without thinking of him in this kitchen, beating eggs and flipping bread fried to a perfect golden brown.

Her anger cranked up another notch.

She glanced over her shoulder. Reid was glowering at her and it frustrated her even more.

'Maybe I just want a quick tumble,' she said, her cheeks burning, her pulse throbbing wildly at her temples. 'A few hours of *goddamn* pleasure. You ever thought of that?'

She turned back to stare blindly at the shelves. *Where was the bloody vanilla?*

'Seeing as how *you* don't fancy me,' she said, not bothering to turn this time because his rejection of her still stung, 'why shouldn't I look somewhere else?'

'Don't *fancy* you?' His voice was deep and dark, brimming with annoyance.

Before she could blink his hands were on her shoulders and she was spun around and pushed hard against the pantry door. His face loomed up close, white-hot flame burning in the blue eyes that raked her face. His breathing was husky, his chest heaving.

'I can't get you out of my head,' he muttered, each word puffing his breath in her face, disturbing her fringe. 'If you had any idea how much I wanted to rip your underwear off *with my teeth* the other night you'd run screaming from this house.'

Trinity's heart rate skyrocketed as his grip on her upper arms tightened and his lips slammed onto hers.

It was a kiss that took. That ruled. That owned.

Possessive. Demanding. His tongue thrusting into her mouth, taking the kiss deeper. The graze of his beard marked her face, prickling *everywhere*.

She felt it *everywhere*.

She was a slave to the sensation. A slave to the onslaught.

His thigh jammed between her legs, high and hard, grinding against the apex of her thighs. She moaned as her aching flesh revelled in the delicious torture, rubbing herself shamelessly against him.

But as quickly as it had started, it was over. His mouth was gone. The kiss was done. His hands still gripped her arms though, his thigh still jammed between her legs.

They stared at each other for long moments, nothing but ragged breathing between them. His mouth was wet and swollen, the white-hot flame in his gaze burning brighter. He grabbed her hand and shoved it on the hard bulge pressing against the zipper of his bike leathers.

'This is *not*,' he whispered, 'about me not fancying you.'

He let her go abruptly and stormed out of the room.

Trinity's legs wobbled for a beat or two before they lost the ability to keep her upright and she slid down the pantry door to the floor, her fingers pressed to her mouth, her mind wiped of coherent thought.

As dramatic as the kiss had been, it seemed to have cleared the air between them a little. At least they both knew where they stood. He *did* fancy her. And she fancied him. They were attracted to one another.

But that was as far as it was going to go.

He hadn't articulated that part exactly but the things he *hadn't* said were just as potent as what he had.

Strangely enough, despite her level of sexual frustration, Trinity was okay with that. Knowing Reid fancied her had done wonders for her ego even if she struggled to wrap her head around the why of it.

Knowing he wasn't going to act on it was something she could live with.

Reid was trying hard to do the right thing. The guy had a strong sense of ethics, which wasn't something she'd seen in a lot of men. Frankly, it was admirable as hell.

And what was one more thing she couldn't have?

It didn't mean she didn't want to get out of Reid's house as soon as possible though. She had enough money saved to start looking for somewhere to live and moving out was probably best all round.

Denial was easier when temptation wasn't staring you in the face day in, day out.

But, as Trinity soon discovered, it wasn't going to be as easy as she'd thought. It seemed late November through December was a busy time of year. Everyone wanted to be in new rentals by Christmas and real-estate agents had nothing on their books—nothing she could reasonably afford anyway that was within a ten-kilometre radius of the hospital because that was non-negotiable.

She'd seen Oscar deteriorate too quickly to be blasé about their address.

About a dozen realtors today had told her that she probably wouldn't get anything now until the new year. She was on a wait list with them but she didn't hold out much hope.

'Damn it,' she swore at the phone as she hung up from yet another *Sorry, try us in January* response.

'Problem?'

Trinity looked over her shoulder, her pulse doing its usual tap dance at Reid's voice. He was in the office doorway, taking up all the space as he shrugged out of his jacket, his T-shirt pulling taut across his abs.

'Apparently trying to get a place to rent in December is like trying to find the pot of gold at the end of the rainbow.' She turned back to the desk and scrubbed another realtor off the list. 'I've been getting no room at the inn for two whole days now.'

'I…didn't realise you were planning on leaving so soon.'

She heard the frown in his voice and sensed him approaching. He sat on the chair positioned beside the desk so she couldn't not look at him.

'I have enough saved up, thanks to you, and I'd hoped to be in our own place by Christmas. Our *first* Christmas in a place that's just ours. Oscar's never had that.'

He nodded. 'That's fair enough. But you know you're more than welcome to stay on here. Pops and I do a pretty mean Christmas. He loves buying the biggest tree and stuffing presents under it. He's like a big kid. And we ignore the fact it's forty degrees outside and have the full turkey and pudding with all the trimmings. Pops would love to have you both here.'

Pops? What about him?

'I would too.'

His smile was genuine and Trinity had to admit it sounded like nirvana. The only Christmas lunch they'd had in the last five years that hadn't been in hospital had been at a soup kitchen. 'Yes, but I'm reliably informed it'll probably be January before more rentals become available.'

'So?' He shrugged and it stretched out the confines of his T-shirt. 'Stay till January.'

It seemed so simple. So straightforward. But they'd impinged on Reid's hospitality long enough. And then there was the elephant in the room. 'It sounds great but…it's probably for the best if we move as soon as possible, don't you think?'

The gaze that met hers was frank. It was the first time either had made reference to their attraction and he didn't bother to pretend he didn't know what she was talking about.

'I'm sure we can both survive each other's company until the new year,' he said with a dry twist in his tone. 'And think how much better off your financial position would be by then.'

Trinity had to admit he made a good point. About her finances. She wasn't entirely sure about the other. The urge to straddle him right now, feel the soft leather of his bike pants against her inner thighs, feel him driving into her, was so strong she returned her attention to the computer.

'Look, I assume you're on some kind of wait list with some agencies?'

'Yes.'

'Well, if something comes up then take it. Pops and I will help you move. If not, stay here with us. It's absolutely fine. No pressure either way, okay?'

If anybody had told her the first time she'd clapped eyes on Reid that this big, bearded, tattooed lumberjack of a guy was good and kind and decent, she wouldn't have believed it. But he'd proved her wrong at every turn.

She glanced at him. 'Okay. Thank you.'

He gave a brief nod of acknowledgement then hauled himself out of the chair and out of reach.

The first of December arrived. It was hot and sticky, a storm was brewing but Eddie, Reid and Oscar paid that no heed as they went out and bought the biggest Christmas tree they could find.

They'd picked him up from school and taken him to a farm on the outskirts of the city where they sold fresh trees. It was a male bonding experience, Reid had insisted in a big gruff lumberjack voice, which had made Oscar laugh and Trinity go a little weak below her belly button.

The fact Reid looked as if he spent all day chopping down trees with a giant axe only added to the weakness.

The guys walked through the door at six in the evening with the biggest tree Trinity had ever seen in her life. It stood a foot higher than Reid— at least.

'I picked it, Mummy,' Oscar announced, his

chest puffing out as Trinity wondered how in hell they were going to get it through the door.

They managed and it fitted perfectly in the living room with its raked ceiling.

'Can we decorate it now?'

Oscar hopped from foot to foot, utterly beside himself with excitement. 'Sure thing, little dude,' Reid said and they fist-bumped. 'You'll need to give me a hand with the lights first though. They have to go on before everything else.'

'I'll get the music,' Eddie volunteered.

Bing Crosby crooned from the sound system as the tree took shape from plain green foliage to a sparkly, tinselled, beribboned, glorious mishmash.

Oscar had been given the responsibility of decorating all the lower branches to where he could reach and Trinity and Reid had decorated the top branches. The tree was, consequently, a little unbalanced. Trinity had tried to subtly encourage Oscar to spread things out and stop him from using *all* the ornaments.

It wasn't, after all, *their* tree.

But Eddie had said, 'Nonsense,' and knelt down to help Oscar pile on some more.

Trinity was sure window decorators all around

the world were probably dropping into dead faints but she'd never seen anything more messily beautiful than this tree.

'And now, young sir,' Eddie said, pulling a star out of a battered box. It looked crazed with age and fragile. 'My wife and I bought this on our honeymoon at the Christmas markets in Vienna over fifty years ago. Would you like to do the honour?'

Oscar stared at the huge golden ornament with wonder. 'Yes, please,' he said on a reverent whisper.

'Here, little dude.' Reid picked him up and hoisted Oscar onto his shoulders, his skinny little legs either side of Reid's neck. He took the star from Eddie then handed it up to Oscar.

'Be very careful,' Trinity murmured, her heart in her mouth as she watched in trepidation the fragile family heirloom change hands.

'There you go,' Reid said as he stood close to the tree and tipped forward slightly. 'Put it on top, there.'

Trinity's chest just about exploded at the picture before her. Oscar, his face serious, his tongue sticking out of the side of his mouth in concentration. Reid, one hand on Oscar's back, the other on a thigh, holding him firmly, his confidence that her son was capable of the honour sitting Oscar a little taller.

They looked good together. Like father and son. Her heart squeezed painfully. This was the kind of life Oscar deserved. Bing Crosby singing carols. Heirlooms.

Family.

'Merry Christmas, Mummy,' Oscar said.

Trinity blinked out of her reverie to find Oscar and Reid facing her. His hands hung on around Reid's neck now, one little finger absently stroking the scratchiness of Reid's beard.

'Merry Christmas, Oscar,' she said, her heart filled to bursting.

'Thank you,' she mouthed to Reid.

He smiled and set Oscar down.

CHAPTER FIFTEEN

Two WEEKS LATER, with no word from an agency, Trinity had resigned herself to waiting until the new year to find a place to live. But that was moot right now as she sat in Oscar's school hall with Reid and Eddie, watching Oscar's class perform 'Jingle Bells' at the Christmas concert.

School would be over in a few days but for now the students were singing their little hearts out. The hall had been decorated in tinsel and fairy lights and all the classes would be performing tonight.

Trinity was hyperaware of Reid sitting next to her. They were sitting on plastic chairs jammed close together so they were shoulder to shoulder, thigh to thigh. They might not have been had he not been so big and broad, but he was and they were. The heat of his leg through the thin fabric of her Christmas dress was *very* distracting.

Yes. A dress. She'd seen it in the local op shop window and had decided, for the first time in a long time, to splurge on something for *her*. It had been brand new, the label still attached, but had only cost ten dollars. It was red with shoestring straps, a sweetheart neckline, fitted bodice and an A-line skirt that swished around her thighs. It came to just below her knee, and encircling the hem was a cherry and holly leaves motif.

It had been love at first sight.

She'd even gone to a hair salon known for its budget prices and had a good couple of inches chopped off as well as some layers cut in around her face. The woman had even used the hair straightener to add some curls.

Between the dress and the hair she'd spent fifty dollars but she felt like a freaking princess.

A guilty twinge about spending money on herself had spoilt things a little but she had quite a nest egg now and she knew the other parents would be dressing up tonight. She didn't want to wear something ill-fitting and old. She didn't want to look poor.

She didn't want to *embarrass* Oscar either.

Or that was what she'd told herself. The fact that Reid had done a double take and stared at her when she'd come down the stairs had been a bonus.

'Doesn't Mummy look pretty, Reid?' Oscar had said.

And he'd looked at her glossed-up mouth as he had that day he'd kissed her in the pantry and said, 'She does indeed, little dude.'

Butterflies fluttered in her belly just thinking about it now.

The song came to an end and the applause was instantaneous. Oscar grinned at her from the stage, wiping a hand across his runny nose. Other parents might have been embarrassed by the action but it caused a much more visceral reaction in Trinity.

Ever since it had started a few days ago, she'd been on edge about it. Waiting for the roller coaster to begin. For the fever to start, for the lethargy to set in. Poised to whisk him off to hospital at the first sign of his condition worsening.

She'd checked on him half a dozen times the last few nights. Oscar had decided last week that he *did* want his own room. Because Raymond had one. But with the development of this sniffle she wished he were still in with her.

He'd been fine though—so far. No temps or malaise. No croaky voice or cough or wheeze. No telling her he didn't feel well. Just a clear runny nose that hadn't seemed to bother him in the least.

Normally he would have crashed into a heap by now. But he'd been bright-eyed and bushy-tailed. Energetic and bubbly, excited about Christmas and having some play dates with Raymond over the holidays.

Trinity had begun to hope that he was over the worst of his prematurity and his lungs were now big enough and strong enough to cope with a sniffle or two.

That truly would be a Christmas miracle.

Two hours later they were home after the concert and Reid was banging a nail into the front door to hang the wreath Oscar had made at school. It looked cheap and childish amongst the posh neighbourhood wreaths but Reid treated it as if it had been bought from Harrods.

'That,' Reid proclaimed, standing back to admire Oscar's creation, 'is the most awesome wreath I have seen. Best in the street, don't you reckon, Pops?'

Eddie nodded. 'The best ever.'

Oscar stood a foot taller and Trinity wanted to cry. These two guys were so *good* for him. Something, somewhere had been smiling on her the day she'd run off those thugs.

'Okay.' She clapped her hands. 'Time for bed.'

Trinity expected resistance. She didn't think Oscar would—*could*—go to sleep after all the excitement. He'd been on such a high all day. But he went happily and was out like a light as soon as his head hit the pillow. She smiled, snapping off his lamp and kissing his forehead.

A prickle of anxiety needled her at its warmth but she gave herself a shake. It was warm. *Not* hot. Not *feverish*.

He was fine.

And the fact she had a doctor in the house was even more reassuring.

She paused at his door for one last look before leaving it slightly ajar and went downstairs. She made three cups of coffee, one each for Reid and Eddie, who were watching *Carols by Candlelight* on the television, and one for her, which she took outside to her favourite spot—the love seat.

Trinity swung idly, a smile on her lips, her thoughts full of the concert and Oscar's delight at being involved. It was as tranquil as ever out here. The night filled with the promise of Christmas. That intangible change in the atmosphere that infected everything and everyone as the big day approached.

She hummed 'Jingle Bells' to herself and smiled some more.

She didn't know how long she sat outside. A long time. The night was gorgeous and it seemed fitting to be out here thanking her lucky stars for the position she was in right now. Plus, she didn't want to take her dress off just yet. It was so nice to feel *female* for a night, she was loath to bring it to an end.

There was also a vague churn of restlessness inside her. The heat in Reid's gaze tonight had been unsettling, stirring up things she'd been trying to suppress. There was no way her body was in a state to sleep just yet.

At some stage the television noises cut out and a minute later the back door was sliding open.

'I thought I'd find you out here.' His low voice carried to her easily on the night.

Goose bumps swept from her nape all the way down her spine. The churn kicked up a notch. The swing rocked as he sat beside her, closer than he usually did. It was still a respectable distance away but her body was so in tune to him.

The churn went into overdrive.

He was still in the trousers and dress shirt he'd worn to the concert, his hair slicked back with some kind of product rather than just pushed messily back off his forehead. She'd never seen him so formal. But even all dressed up, wearing the same kind of clothes as the other men at the concert tonight, there was still something…*untamed* about him.

Maybe it was the beard. Maybe it was the tats beneath that very respectable shirt. Maybe it was those lumberjack shoulders testing the limits of the seams.

Whatever it was, she hadn't been the only one who'd noticed. He'd turned heads.

'That was a great night,' he said, taking over the motion of the swing with his foot.

She glanced at him and smiled. 'Yes,' she murmured before turning back to contemplate the night again. They sat in companionable silence for a few moments.

'You look beautiful tonight.'

Trinity blinked, startled at his husky compliment. Her pulse quickened. No one had ever called her beautiful. Not even Bri. He'd told her she was cute and had used words like *mighty fine*.

But never beautiful. It seemed like a much deeper compliment. More measured. More meaningful.

The kind of compliment a *man* would give.

'Oh…thank you.' She swallowed, suddenly conscious of the lip gloss she'd slicked on and the curls in her hair. 'You don't scrub up too badly yourself.'

She'd kept her voice light, his low chuckle feathering down her arms.

'That's a great outfit you're wearing.'

Trinity glanced down at herself. 'It's just a dress.'

'*That* is not just a dress.' His eyes raked over her, taking in her hair and her cleavage and the fall of the fabric over her legs. Everything tingled in their wake. 'That's like…a walking advert for Christmas. Red looks good on you.'

His compliments were going to her head. And other parts of her body. Warmth stole into her cheeks. Heat flared between her legs.

'You should wear more clothes like that.'

This conversation was dicing pretty close to the wind as far as their attraction went but Trinity didn't seem to be able to help herself around him.

And he'd started it.

'Like what? Dresses?'

'No, I mean things that aren't two sizes too big for you or hang like a sack.'

'I don't deliberately buy them like that,' she said waspishly. 'I've had most of my clothes a long time and I've lost weight in the last five years. I haven't been able to afford to buy new ones so I've just…made do.'

'How much weight?'

The question was fired back at her, a wrinkle drawing his brows together. Obviously it had come from Reid the doctor.

'A couple of dress sizes.'

He nodded, thoughtful for a moment. 'You don't splash out on yourself much, do you?'

Trinity fingered the dress. 'This is it.'

'Well, you should never take it off,' he said, a grin on his face and in his voice as he dragged his eyes off her. 'It's your turn now to say how a respectable doctor should be wearing more of these kinds of clothes.' He pulled at his shirt with a disdainful curl to his lips.

'Fishing for compliments?' she teased. Her breath hitching at how easy he was to tease.

'Maybe.'

Trinity shook her head. The urge to stroke the front of his shirt, to feel the fabric and the muscles beneath, was surprisingly strong. 'I like what you wear.'

He turned his head to look at her, clearly surprised at her admission. 'Do you, now?'

It was on the tip of Trinity's tongue to say, *Especially when you're mowing*, but she dragged her gaze away, returning her attention to the stars, not willing to give too much away.

They lapsed into silence again. Nothing but the squeak of the swing between them.

'Did you see that kid tonight in the back row pick his nose during "Silent Night"?'

Trinity pressed her lips together to stop the threatening laughter. 'Yes.'

He didn't bother to suppress it. He laughed into the night, deep and throaty, and she joined him. She'd felt a shudder of silent laughter ripple through Reid's shoulders at the time and had bit her own cheek to stop from doing likewise but neither of them felt similarly constrained now.

In fact Trinity laughed so hard she almost had tears running down her face.

When their laughter slowly faded they were half turned towards each other and Reid said, 'Oscar was brilliant though.'

She nodded. 'Yes. He was.' Without any thought

she reached her hand across and squeezed his arm. The muscle tensed beneath her touch and she quickly withdrew.

'Thank you,' she said, ignoring the hammer of her heartbeat to say what had to be said. 'Just… *thank you*…from the bottom of my heart. For you and Eddie coming tonight and for hanging the wreath.' She shook her head, overwhelmed by Reid's generosity. 'I'm just so—'

The swift, hot press of his mouth cut her off. It stole her breath and robbed her brain of any thought other than *yes*.

And *more*.

He kept it brief though, withdrawing as quickly as he had lunged, causing her to almost pitch forward at the abrupt disconnect. She blinked at him, her mouth tingling, her lungs burning as if she'd just run a hundred metres in under ten seconds.

'Sorry.' He grimaced. 'I've wanted to do that ever since you walked down the stairs tonight wearing that lip gloss.'

Trinity blinked. 'Oh.' She drew in a shaky breath. 'So…we're disregarding the line tonight?'

'Goddamn it,' he muttered, *thunking* his head back against the seat cushion, his gaze fixed on the stars. 'I hate that line. I swear trying to do the right thing is *killing* me.'

The crazy low rumble of his voice scraped along her nerve endings. She couldn't believe what he was saying.

'It doesn't matter what I do or what I tell myself, I can't stop thinking about you and then I go to bed and, *God...*' He groaned and rolled his head along the cushion to face her. 'I dream about you. These...erotic dreams that wake me in the middle of the night and I'm so hard for you and then you wear this dress tonight and I swear I'm going to go to hell for kissing you just now but—'

It was Trinity's turn to kiss him, to cut him off, to feel the prick of his beard and taste the coffee on his breath.

He wanted her. He dreamed about her. He couldn't stop thinking about her. If he was going to hell then she was going along for the ride.

She didn't know what that meant for them long term; she didn't care. She needed this tonight. They both did.

Without any coherent thought she was turning, twisting, sliding a leg over his lap, sending the love seat into a rocking frenzy as she grabbed his shoulders and straddled him.

He groaned and muttered, *'Trinity,'* against her mouth as her dress flared out over his lap and his hands found the smooth bare skin of her ass.

Trinity ploughed her fingers into his hair as he squeezed her cheeks and everything inside her clenched tight. She was so hot, so wet, so needy.

So ready.

Her underwear met the zip of his trousers and the bulge beneath and she moaned—*loud*—her head falling back, the kiss abandoned to the pleasure of rubbing her aching flesh in just the right spot.

'Okay,' he said, his lips at her neck, his beard scratching *so damn good* at the sensitive hollows. 'I think we need to move this inside because I'm about to relieve you of this dress and the neighbours might get a show they hadn't bargained for.'

There was a smile in his voice as he ground against her and Trinity gasped at how good it felt.

'I thought you said I should never take it off.'

'I lied.'

Then he picked her up, still straddling him, and strode into the house.

CHAPTER SIXTEEN

FIVE MINUTES LATER Trinity found Reid in his bedroom, lamplight bathing him in a soft glow. She'd checked on Oscar and now here she was. He was barefoot and had undone the buttons of his shirt and the top button of his trousers but had taken neither of them off.

How could a partially dressed man be just as sexy as a completely naked one?

She glimpsed the tats that ran under the ridge of his collarbones and was looking forward to exploring them all.

Later…

'Take off your dress.'

His bold command was as visceral as if he'd stroked his hand along her belly. He hadn't moved. He hadn't come nearer or tried to touch her but it *felt* like it.

Quickly, hands trembling behind her, she unzipped. The shoestring straps fell off her shoulders and in one shrug the dress had pooled around her feet. She wasn't wearing a bra. All that stood between her and naked was faded pink underwear.

'My God…' he muttered under his breath, the air hissing out of his lungs as his gaze fell to her bare breasts.

'Take off your shirt.'

Her request was tremulous with desire, far less steady than his had been. But he stopped her breath as she watched him strip out of it. She feasted her eyes on the acres of tanned and tatted flesh before her just as he was feasting his eyes on her.

She admired the musculature *and* the art, her heart belting along as his gaze roamed over every inch of her body.

Her nipples puckered tight as he stared at them as if they were his own personal toys.

Trinity didn't know who was supposed to make the first move now. She didn't care either. She only cared about his skin on hers. His mouth on hers. The bulge behind his zipper filling her up.

Enough looking. She needed touching.

She needed it *now*.

She stumbled towards him as if on autopilot. They met somewhere in the middle, at the foot of his bed, her calf brushing the edge of the mattress. She twined her arms around his neck, rising up on tiptoe, her breasts brushing his chest as she sought his mouth, whimpering when she found it, moaning when their lips clashed and clung and opened.

She kissed him deep and hard and wet. She kissed him fast. She kissed him thorough. She kissed him all the ways she knew and all the ways she'd never known. Pressing herself to him, forgetting to breathe, forgetting to think.

'Slow down,' he whispered, against her lips. 'We've got all night.'

But she didn't want to wait all night. She didn't want to wait another *second*. She wanted him inside her. She *needed* him inside her.

Her knee slid onto the bed and she half pulled, half dragged him down to the mattress with her, groping for his fly, desperate to hold him in her hand again, to guide him to where she needed him most.

His lips buzzed her neck, his beard prickling, beading her nipples to unbearable tightness as her hand found the zipper and yanked. Her pulse was like a freight train in her head as she reached inside, her hand finding exactly what she needed.

He was full and thick and Trinity gripped him—hard—stroking up and down the length of him. He was like forged steel wrapped in rose petals and he groaned, deep and low, his forehead jammed to her temple as she kept up the pace.

But she was too damn restricted to do what she really wanted to do. Too many clothes. 'Off,' she said, panting in his ear as she used her spare hand to push at the waistband of his trousers where they covered his ass. 'Take your pants off.'

He didn't argue, just rolled on his back and wriggled out of the offending articles. Trinity watched, her gaze glued to the jut of his erection—thick and perfect. And then he was back, looming over her on all fours, his hair wild, his tattoos framing him perfectly. He slid an arm under her body and scooped her up the bed until they were fully on the mattress, yanking her underwear off and stripping them down her legs in one easy move.

He sat back on his haunches admiring what he saw. She wasn't embarrassed by such a thorough inspection; she was beyond that, his heated gaze only cranking her fever higher. He looked at her as if he wanted to devour every inch of her and couldn't decide where to start.

She knew where *she* wanted to start. His erection sprang from the nest of hair between his legs, proud and potent. She levered herself up on her elbows, reached for the hard jut of him, but he caught her hand, kissed it, shook his head. 'Patience,' he murmured.

Trinity fell back against the mattress, her hair flying as frustration burned through her veins like sulphur. Her breasts jiggled with the movement and Reid's gaze zeroed in on them. A light that was almost feral, totally befitting his lumberjack masculinity, flared in his eyes and he was on her, his head dipping to claim one nipple as his hand slid onto the other.

'Oh… God…' She moaned, arched her back, ploughed her hand into his hair as he settled his body against the mattress, his tongue repeatedly flicking back and forth over the hard nub.

She felt a corresponding twinge in the hard nub between her legs as if his tongue were down there, flicking back and forth. Down where she needed him to be. Where it roared and ached.

Where she wanted the hard, thick length of him to fill and stretch and burn. To rock and pound. To drive her into the bed until she clamped tight around him. To remind her she was a *woman*.

In the most base way possible.

She needed that.

'Reid,' she muttered, dragging all the discombobulated parts of herself together, pulling at his hair, dragging him off. 'I need you *inside* me.'

His mouth was wet from the havoc he'd been creating. 'All in good time,' he muttered, his head dipping again to reclaim a nipple begging for the hot suck of his mouth and the delicious burn of his beard.

Trinity forced herself to calm, to breathe, to slow down. To let him have it his way, to let him explore. But her pulse would not be slowed, nor would the tremble in her hands or the deeper tremble in her body.

It was seismic. And not willing to be ignored.

Screw it. *The time was now.*

She yanked on his hair. *Hard.* He didn't even wince; there was too much lumberjack about him for that. If anything a flare of something lit his eyes as if maybe he'd enjoyed it.

A corresponding flare lit deep in her body.

'Now.' Her gaze locked with his, her breath ragged. 'I swear to God, Reid, I need you in me now.'

He didn't say anything for long moments, his

gaze searching hers. Then he reached over her to his bedside table, yanking out the drawer, and pulled out a foil packet.

Tearing it quickly with his teeth, he had himself sheathed in five seconds flat before he loomed over her, supporting himself on his forearms as he settled between her legs. She opened for him, her heart hammering, her breath chugging in and out.

She wanted it *so* bad.

He flexed his hips and she cried out at the fullness of that first thick nudge. 'Are you okay?' he asked, easing back the pressure.

He was big, she knew that from what she'd already seen of him and how he'd filled her hand, and she was out of practice but women *were* designed to stretch.

'God, yes,' she said, clamping her hand tight on his ass, shamelessly rotating her hips.

He slid all the way in then. Slow and steady and sure. A long low groan spilling from his throat as he eased in to the hilt. 'God,' he said, his voice a husky rumble, his forehead resting on hers. 'You feel good.'

Trinity let out a shaky breath, shifting against

the mattress to better accommodate him. 'You feel *incredible.*'

He grunted something unintelligible as he withdrew—slowly, slowly—his forehead still planted on hers, then eased back in again just as slowly.

She tightened her hand on his ass. 'Faster.'

'No,' he said as he withdrew and entered again, so slow she could feel every wet inch of herself pulsing around every hard inch of him.

He did it a few more times, stoking the embers deep inside her pelvis, slowly breathing them to life. But they were out of kilter with the frenzy in her nerves and the fever in her blood. She didn't want embers, she wanted *flames.* 'Damn it, Reid, faster.'

'So bossy,' he chuckled as his hips delivered more torturously slow thrusts.

'Please,' she whispered, clamping down around him and pushing him out as he withdrew, expelling him faster.

She gasped and he groaned at the action, his forehead falling into the crook of her neck as he hunched into it more, adding an extra punch to entry right at the end as he reached her limit.

She moaned at the quick spasmodic jab. The coarse rasp of his beard at her throat intensified the sensation, streaking like a bolt of lightning between her legs.

But it still wasn't enough. *'Please.'*

He dragged his head off her neck, the liquid blue heat of his gaze locking with hers as he held himself buried deep inside her. The pressure was so intense she could barely breathe.

'You deserve a man to love you right, Trinity. To take it slow. To worship you. Let me do that.'

Crazy tears pricked at the backs of her eyes. Even in something so base and elemental as sex, Reid was looking out for her. It was sweet and kind. So at odds with his lumberjack physicality but so typical of the gentle man she'd come to know.

But she didn't want that. Not right *now*.

She didn't want slow and steady. She wanted it hard. She wanted it dirty. She wanted it to hurt *so damn good*. She wanted to feel the ache for days to come. She wanted to leave this bed having had her world thoroughly rocked.

To have a memory she could bring out in the future if things got tough again.

And she knew he could give that to her. She had no doubt he could be a considerate and generous lover but she wanted the lumberjack she knew he was holding back. She could feel it in the tremble of his biceps and the hard clench of his glute beneath her hand.

'I'm not some fragile chick who needs kid gloves,' she said, her cheeks flushed, her pulse hammering at her temples and throbbing deep inside her where she gripped him. *I'm tough.*'

He chuckled. 'You don't think I know that?'

'Then why are you treating me like I'm going to break?' she demanded. 'I don't want you to *worship* me, damn it. I want you to *possess* me.'

He stared at her for long moments. His gaze searching, assessing. She saw the moment his mind was made up, the sudden clarity followed by his swift withdrawal from her body.

She opened her mouth to protest but in the blink of an eye he'd flipped her over, wrapped his hand in her hair, dragged her right hip up and used his thigh to push her right knee into a bend, completely exposing her to his view.

Trinity's heart rate careened crazily in her chest as his erection prodded her slick entrance again but there was nothing slow and steady about this penetration; it was fast and quick, ripping a cry from her throat and a grunt of satisfaction from him.

He tugged on her hair, forcing her head off the bed and her back into an arch, sparks of electricity showering from her scalp all the way down her spine. 'Like that?' he whispered in her ear, his beard prickling at her neck and shoulder.

She panted. '*Yes*. God, yes. More.'

'Good,' he grunted and gave her more.

Hard and fast and relentless.

He held her like that, one hand wrapped in her hair, keeping her head up and her back arched as his mouth ravaged the muscle that sloped from her neck to her shoulder and his hips hammered into her from behind. It was hard and intense and perfect and all she was capable of was moaning and writhing until the hand he had on her hip slid around to her front and ploughed through the slickness between her legs, finding the hard knot of nerves.

'Come for me,' he demanded in her ear, low and ragged.

And she did. The pressure that had been building blew out in one hot flare and she came. Loud and long. Bucking against him as he mercilessly drove into her over and over again.

'*Trinity.*'

He groaned into her neck as the piston of his

hips suddenly stopped. One second. Two. And then he bellowed his own release, muffling it in her shoulder as his hips bucked again and he rocked them towards the light together.

They lay unmoving for a long time in the aftermath, their bodies still intimately connected. Reid had collapsed against her, his weight pressing her to the bed, his mouth pressed to her nape, sweat slicking them together.

And she revelled in it.

Trinity had known she'd shatter. Hell, she'd *craved* it. But in a physical sense only. She hadn't been prepared to be broken into a thousand pieces *emotionally*. She hadn't been prepared for the gates of her heart to break open too and for love to flow in.

She hadn't been prepared for love at all.

But, as they lay in a sweaty heap, she knew it had happened anyway, could feel the burden of it sink to the pit of her belly.

She was in love with Reid Hamilton. It wasn't lust or gratitude or friendship. It was the deep and totally gut-wrenching abyss of unrequited love.

She'd wanted him to remind her she was a

woman. She just hadn't expected that taking Reid into her body would make her *his* woman.

And he could *never, ever* know.

CHAPTER SEVENTEEN

REID SHIVERED AND his groin tightened as Trinity traced the feathers of his eagle wings with her index fingers. She was firmly snuggled into his side, her hand reaching across to his opposite arm. The tattoo was on his back but the wings stretched all the way around to brush the tops of his biceps.

It was two in the morning and they'd already had sex three times. The second two not as hurried as the first. She *had* let him love her slow and easy the next time. And the third time, he'd headed down her body and shown her there were many, *many* ways to make a woman call out to God.

They were sated—for now—as they lay in each other's arms. His hand was stroking from her ass to her hip and back again as they drifted in the aftermath. He'd always enjoyed the post-coital haze, floating in his own bone-deep satisfaction, knowing whoever he was with was floating in hers.

But this was different. There was no exit strategy forming in his head as per usual. Lying here with Trinity was…grounding. And not in a bad way. Ever since she and Oscar had moved in he'd felt…settled. Not something he'd experienced since before his parents got divorced.

He'd forgotten how good it felt.

'You like them?' he murmured, prying heavy eyelids open as her exploring fingers brushed down his biceps.

She wrinkled her nose slightly as her gaze followed the path of her finger. 'I'm not a big fan of tattoos, I have to admit, but they suit the whole lumberjack thing you've got going on.'

That surprised a laugh out of Reid. *'Lumberjack?'*

'Yes.' She smiled as she levered herself up on one elbow, looking down at him. 'The whole big, macho, bearded biker thing. All you need is a flannel shirt and a big old axe and you'd be the real deal.'

Reid shook his head, amused at the thought. A lock of hair had fallen forward over her shoulder and he pushed it back. 'Any particular reason why you're not into them?'

She sighed. 'Those couple of years on the streets…tats were usually a signal that you were someone who shouldn't be messed with. That was their point, I guess. I learned to be wary.'

Reid had known a lot of badass guys in the military who had been fully aware of how intimidating their tats could be and had revelled in it. He just appreciated the art.

'And yet you have one,' he murmured, his fingers tracing the ladybird tattoo on her right hip he'd thoroughly checked out on his way down earlier.

'Brian talked me into it. The place we went to was a real dive. I'm surprised I didn't get hepatitis. If I can ever afford the luxury of having it lasered off, I will.'

There was a grimness to her voice. 'Well, I like it,' he teased, to lighten the mood, his fingers stroking the offending piece of artwork.

'It takes me back to a dark time in my life every time I see it.' She shuddered. 'I hate being reminded of it all the time.'

Reid couldn't fault her reasons. Hell, he understood them. All of his tattoos had been acquired during his tours of duty in the Middle East. A lot of bad memories there.

But good ones also.

'Sometimes,' he said, picking up the same, persistent lock of hair he'd pushed back earlier, toying with it, 'those reminders can be good.'

She regarded him for long moments. 'Is that what yours do?' Her fingers had shifted to his mouth now, tracing around the line where his beard rimmed his lips. 'Remind you of your time in the military?'

'Yeah.'

'And that's…good?' She frowned. 'I wouldn't have thought you'd want to be reminded of it.'

He shut his eyes as her fingers fluttered like moth wings over his lips. 'There are some bad memories,' he murmured, his eyes drifting open, fixing on hers. 'Things that still give me nightmares from time to time. Soldiers we lost. People I couldn't help. The *children* in the villages… But more than anything it reminds me that we did good over there. Every time people talk about the disaster of it, I know we did *good* as well. I need that.'

She nodded slowly and it felt as if she understood. Then she lowered her mouth and kissed him, sweet and slow and full of something deep and earnest he couldn't quite put his finger on. A kiss that seemed to say sorry and thank you and…goodbye?

She pulled away, her tawny gaze heated, her mouth wet from his and he wanted to crush her to him so there wouldn't be a goodbye.

'You don't ever think of going back?' she asked, her voice husky.

'No.' His hand slid to her ass and he squeezed. 'I'm feeling remarkably good about being home, actually.'

'Oh, yeah?' She smiled. 'That doesn't sound very rolling stone of you.'

He shrugged. 'What can I say? You're a good influence. I think I'm feeling more settled in my old age.'

'Really?' There was an odd little hitch to her voice, but then his fingers *were* trailing down the slope of her buttocks.

'I might celebrate with a new tattoo, actually.'

She slid her knee forward over his thighs and his fingers slid into the slick heat between her legs. 'Oh?' she said, her eyes fluttering closed as he explored.

'A big axe.' He grinned, his gaze roaming her

face, enjoying her bliss. 'Embedded right in the centre of my chest.'

Her eyes opened and he tapped the area near his heart as his thumb grazed the hard little nub between her legs. She leaned in, kissed the spot, then slid her leg all the way over his hips and straddled him.

Trinity woke with a start, disorientated, a few hours later. Something had disturbed her but she didn't know what.

'Mummy!'

Oscar. Crying. Distressed.

'Oscar?'

She was lying with Reid spooned behind her and she had to push his arm out of the way to leap from the bed.

'What's wrong?' Reid asked, his voice sleepy and confused.

But she wasn't thinking about Reid. 'I'm coming,' she called out, her heart beating rapidly as the all-too-familiar sense of dread flooded her system. Conscious of being naked, she groped for her discarded dress and threw it over her head, zipping it up as she hurried out of the door.

Her heart rate almost doubled when Oscar wasn't in his room. *'Oscar!'*

'I'm here, Mummy,' came a plaintive little voice from the direction of her bedroom.

She flew next door to find Oscar standing beside her bed. *'Oscar!'*

'Where were you, Mummy?' he asked as she swept him up in her arms and hugged him to her fiercely.

'What's wrong,' she said, disregarding his question as unimportant right at this moment.

'I don't feel very well.'

Trinity squeezed her eyes shut at his typical understatement. His forehead was burning up and the rest of his body burned beneath the thin cotton of his pyjamas.

She could hear and feel the rattle of his breathing through his chest and the faint end note of a wheeze.

She sat with him on the bed. 'Is it hard to breathe?'

'A little bit,' he confirmed, lying slack in her arms as a weak, moist cough emphasised his condition.

Reid suddenly appeared in the doorway, pretty much as he'd been when she'd first gone to his room. Trousers, top button undone, shirt flapping open. 'Is he okay?' he asked, flipping on the light and advancing into the room.

Trinity shut her eyes against the sudden insult to her pupils. 'No.' She shook her head. 'He's not. I'm going to have to take him to the hospital.'

He crouched before them, placing a hand on Oscar's back. 'He doesn't sound very good and he's definitely got a temp. Does he have any recession?'

She wished she didn't know what Reid was talking about but unfortunately she was all too familiar with medical terminology. Trinity didn't have to look to know that the intercostal spaces between Oscar's ribs would be prominent. That his accessory muscles of respiration would be sucking in, working overtime. They'd need to take his shirt off to confirm but she didn't want to faff around.

'I would bet my life on it.'

'I can get my stethoscope and have a listen?'

Trinity shook her head. It wasn't that she didn't trust his doctoring skills, it just seemed pointless and time wasting when action was what she needed. 'I know how this goes, Reid. He can go from a sniffle to being ventilated in a matter of hours. I just want to get him to hospital.'

'Okay.'

She was grateful he didn't try to override her or tell her to calm down, that she was panicking for no reason as she'd heard too often in the past from people—some of them medical—who just didn't understand.

His faith in her ability to know her own son and his condition, his faith in her motherly instincts, almost undid her. If she hadn't loved him before now, she would have in this moment. But she *could not* indulge in flights of fancy about the two of them *or* the threatening tears.

She was going to need to be extra tough for the days ahead.

He stood. 'I'll drive.'

Trinity blinked at the offer and for one brief moment allowed herself the fantasy of having Reid—the man she loved—by her side throughout the ordeal she knew was about to unfold. Someone to lean on.

But…

It could be a long haul and it wasn't practical for Reid, who had a job and his grandfather to worry about. She'd been living a fantasy here with him and she needed to get back to the real world.

'You can't. There's Eddie,' she said, standing as well.

He shrugged. 'He sleeps like a rock and doesn't usually wake till after six. It's just after two. I'll leave a note but I can stay with you guys for a bit and be back here by then.'

Trinity hated how much she wanted that. How the prospect of him staying with her filled her with yearning. 'But if he—'

'It's fine, Trinity,' he cut in gently, his hand squeezing her forearm. 'Let's just get the little dude to the hospital, okay?'

Trinity swallowed the lump in her throat and nodded.

They were walking into the hospital twenty minutes later, a lethargic Oscar bundled in Trinity's arms. She instantly felt better—safer—the cartoon murals decorating the walls and the staff wearing brightly coloured scrubs as familiar to her as her own breathing.

The triage nurse knew them on sight. 'Oh, dear, what have we got here, Master Oscar?' she said, her smile bright but her eyes knowing as they flicked from mother to son. 'Thought your frequent flyer days were done.'

'So did I.' Trinity grimaced.

'We might pop him straight into the resus cube,' she said, not bothering with the usual triage procedure. Her voice was casually calm but Trinity could read between the lines.

Oscar had crashed in this emergency department too many times for anyone to take any risks.

Trinity nodded, grateful for the assurance, but it didn't stop the worry and fear gnawing at her. Or the despair. After six months of being well she'd desperately hoped that they'd turned a corner with his health so this episode was gutting.

'He's in good hands,' Reid murmured as they followed the nurse.

She nodded, not trusting her voice as an entire catalogue of emotions swamped her. *She* was in good hands with *him*. The warmth of his palm in the small of her back was infinitely assuring and she had to fight the urge to lean against him.

Trinity laid Oscar on the gurney in the resus cube. He didn't protest, just looked at her with resigned, knowing eyes that broke her heart even more than his frightened eyes did. There were kids crying all around them, being combative, clinging to their mothers and protesting interventions. Not Oscar.

In the centre of the activity that had sprung up around him, he lay quiet and accepting. Which was worrying on a whole other level. Trinity fretted that he was becoming exhausted, which could escalate things rapidly.

Reid, standing behind her, squeezed Trinity's shoulder as they undid Oscar's pyjama shirt to stick ECG dots to his chest. His intercostal recession was pronounced, as was his sternal and tracheal recession, the garish white line of his sternotomy scar horrifyingly mobile with each suck of his chest.

There was oxygen then and chest X-rays, intravenous therapy and medications. A whole battery of blood tests. Oscar barely flinched when they stabbed him to insert the IV, and sticking a suction catheter down his nose to get a nasopharyngeal sample raised only a feeble cry.

Doctors came and went. The blood tests were okay. The chest X-ray wasn't too bad. He was holding his own. So many faces she knew. Reassurances given that she trusted, that meant something. But the rapid beeping noise from the monitor formed a terrible backbeat to her concern. She knew a lot of his tachycardia was due to his temperature but it always frightened her to see it belting along at one hundred and sixty beats per minute.

As if surely his heart was going to explode under the pressure or just...stop.

The helplessness was the worst as she stood by the gurney, his little hand furled in hers, alternating between anxiety and hope. Knowing that these doctors and nurses had him, that they were experienced, that they were good at this, that they were fighting for him was immensely reassuring. Then thoughts of how bad this could get crept up on her and she was plunged into despair.

But every time it happened, when the hopelessness seemed overwhelming, Reid's hand would slide onto her shoulder, as if he knew she *needed* it at that precise moment, and it kept her going.

CHAPTER EIGHTEEN

THEY WERE SETTLED in the high dependency unit within two hours. The loud hiss of the high-flow nasal cannula delivering warmed, moist oxygen formed a truly garish white noise in the isolation room, but it was soothing to Trinity's frazzled nerves. As was the now slower, more steady blip of the monitor. Oscar's temp was coming down and his vital signs were less scary.

He was asleep, looking very small and very pale in the big bed, ECG wires, IV tubing and oxygen tubing all criss-crossing his body. He didn't have a shirt on and it was heartening to see that his recession had markedly improved.

The ICU doctor had just been. She was hoping that the high-flow oxygen would be enough to get Oscar over the hump. So was Trinity. Normally, though, his condition would continue to deteriorate and medical interventions would escalate.

But, as always, it was going to be an hour-by-hour thing.

Despite the lack of promises, Trinity felt infinitely better than she had when Oscar's cry had dragged her out of sexually sated slumber.

Was that only a few hours ago?

'I might head off for a bit,' Reid announced as the doctor left. The sun was poking yellow fingers through the partially open blinds. 'I'll clear my day and get back here when I can.'

Trinity frowned. 'It's okay, Reid.' She shook her head. He couldn't just *clear his day*. He had his patients to see. His grandfather to take care of. His own responsibilities.

'You don't have to.'

He smiled. 'I want to.'

'Is this because…?' Trinity was conscious of the nurse in the room. 'You don't have to feel obligated to me because of…what happened earlier.'

Heat rose in her cheeks. She shouldn't be embarrassed considering what she'd done to his body. But there'd been such an abrupt ending to their…tryst, she wasn't sure where they stood.

'Trinity.' His voice was low as his hands smoothed up her arms and he held her gently by the shoulders. 'I want to.'

And then he pulled her in for a hug. She resisted for about two seconds before melting into him, grateful for his broad chest and solid warmth. Grateful that he'd been with her and she hadn't felt so alone. Grateful for his silent support and understanding.

'Thank you,' she said, her voice muffled in his pecs. 'For being here.'

'I'll always be here for you, Trinity.'

Trinity looked at him. She didn't know what that meant. Or the meaning of his deep, searching gaze. And she didn't want to speculate in case her heart took over and came to the wrong conclusion.

She glanced away from the intensity of his eyes to her son. 'He seems to be doing better now, right?' She sought Reid's gaze again, needing him to be Dr Hamilton now, to hear his medical opinion.

'Yes.' He nodded. 'He does. But how are *you* doing?' he asked softly.

How she was doing seemed so frivolous compared to the battle Oscar was facing and Trinity wanted to dismiss it out of hand as she always did in these situations, but his gaze was still so damn intense, demanding she think about herself for a moment.

'I'll...be okay,' she said even if the adrenaline

that had been keeping her going the last few hours had left her shaky and strung out.

'You have to take care of *you*, Trinity. You're no good to Oscar if you're exhausted.'

How many times had she heard that from well-meaning doctors and nurses these past five years? Too many times to count. But to hear it from Reid, the man she loved, who was here to support *her*... To even *have* a support person for a change, to know that someone other than paid strangers *cared*, touched her deeply.

Tears pricked the backs of her eyes and she blinked them away. 'I know,' she said. Because she *did* know, but she also knew that it was a pointless discussion. Her biological drive would always put the welfare of her child first.

The look he gave her told her he knew it too. 'Okay. I'll be back later. Text me if...' His gaze flicked briefly to Oscar then back to her. 'Keep me up to date.'

Trinity nodded, knowing he'd been about to say, *If Oscar deteriorates* and appreciating that he hadn't. And then, much to her surprise, he dropped a light kiss on her mouth before he turned away and left the room.

As if they were in some kind of a *relationship*,

not on the tail end of what had been, essentially, a roll in the hay.

In a daze, Trinity sat by Oscar's bed, her lips tingling from Reid's kiss. The colourful squiggles of the monitor blurred before her eyes as she tried to stop herself from hoping a relationship with Reid was possible.

It was ten at night when Reid strode past the nurses at the central work station, giving them a smile as he headed for Oscar's room. This was his second time back since he'd left this morning.

The first thing he'd done once he'd let himself in the house was ring work and organise cover for the next few days. There were some appointments that had needed rejigging but it had all been sorted.

Trinity had looked so stricken last night. So worried and anxious. He'd been as concerned for her as he had been for Oscar and it was important to him to be there for Trinity. He doubted she'd ever had support during any of Oscar's hospitalisations and he was determined she wasn't going to go through this episode alone.

She—*and Oscar*—had come to mean a whole lot more to him than some kind of charity case.

He *liked* her. Hell, after last night, he hoped she *liked* him too. In the kind of way that involved seeing more of each other.

Still…that wasn't important right now. Oscar getting better was all that mattered.

Reid had brought his grandfather to see Oscar for three hours in the middle of the day. Oscar had pretty much slept all the way through the visit but it had seemed to cheer Trinity up. She'd looked dog-tired with big dark circles under her eyes but Oscar had been holding his own. He was still on the high flow and while they hadn't been able to wean any of the oxygen, it hadn't been increased either.

The results had come in on his naso-pharyngeal aspirate. It was RSV, a common respiratory virus that most people could easily shake but could be devastating to kids like Oscar still suffering the effects of premature lungs. Unfortunately it couldn't be treated with antibiotics, just time and supportive respiratory therapy.

The news hadn't been comforting to Trinity. Apparently Oscar had had it several times before and had been ventilated each time.

Reid could hear the noise of Oscar's high-flow oxygen even before he reached the room. A nurse, sitting at the computer in the room, glanced up at him as he stopped in the open doorway. He glanced at Trinity. Oscar's nearest hand was folded in hers but her head was on the bed and she was sound asleep, her long, low ponytail falling down her back.

The nurse slipped off her stool and headed towards him with a smile.

'How is he?' Reid asked, keeping his voice low, as she drew level.

'We've managed to wean the oxygen a titch,' she murmured.

Relief flooded Reid at the news. Used to operating in high-stress environments, he hadn't realised how worried he'd been. Oscar's reliance on such high levels of oxygen was concerning. Being able to wean it was a positive step forward.

'How's she?'

'I've tried to get her to go and have a proper sleep,' the nurse said with a sigh. 'There are some great pull-out couches in the parents' lounge but she won't leave him.'

Reid nodded. He didn't doubt it for a moment. 'Okay, thanks.'

The nurse left and he advanced into the room,

standing close to the bed, looking down at Trinity. Her face was turned towards Oscar and spotlighted in a pool of light from overhead. The black circles had increased to smudges and the wedge of her cheek looked gaunt and pale.

She looked absolutely exhausted. His belly clenched at the sight and his heart turned over. A rush of love swamped his chest.

Yes…*love.*

God, he'd been fooling himself.

This hadn't been about protection or charity. She'd had an impact on him from that very first day they'd met but he'd ignored it. And she'd been under his skin ever since.

He didn't just *like* her. He *loved* her.

In a couple of months she—and Oscar—had come to mean *everything* to him.

Reid put a hand on the mattress to support legs suddenly not that steady. He should have known when the usual disquiet over staying in one place died down that something was up. But he'd been too busy trying to put her into the friend zone. Too busy mitigating his feelings because of the power imbalance in their relationship. Too busy trying *not to have* feelings for her to really listen to what his body had been telling him.

What his *heart* had been telling him.

He was in love with her.

Pure and simple. Although, not, if she didn't feel the same way.

He knew she was attracted to him. But that wasn't love. And he didn't want to settle for anything less with her. He'd been aware of his feelings for ten seconds but already he knew he wanted the whole shebang. A relationship. A chance to be a father to Oscar. A chance to make them a family.

But whatever he felt at the moment was moot. He couldn't tell her *now*. It all had to go on ice until Oscar was well again and Trinity had space in her head for something other than Oscar's illness.

And, more than that, *right now*, she needed to go and have a proper sleep so she woke up refreshed and not with a kink in her neck.

He crouched beside her chair, one hand sliding on top of her thigh. 'Trinity,' he murmured, pressing a kiss to her cheek.

She stirred, lifted her head, looked quickly at Oscar and the monitor to assure herself he was okay then at him, her brows beetled together. 'Reid?'

'Hey, sleepyhead,' he teased, keeping his voice low.

'I'm sorry.' She wiped a hand across her eyes. 'I must have drifted off.'

'Of course you did. You're exhausted, Trinity.' Neither of them had got much sleep the night before after all…

'What are you doing back here?' she said, ignoring his observation. 'You should be with Eddie.'

'He's pushing out Z's. Just like you.'

'I'm fine.' She shook her head as if clearing a fog. 'It was just a catnap.'

'Trinity.' Reid squeezed her leg gently and she glanced down at it. At his hand on her leg. She stared at it for long moments and he thought he heard her breath hitch before she locked her gaze with his. 'You. Are. *Exhausted.* Go to the parents' lounge and have a proper sleep.' She started to protest but he cut her off. 'I will stay right here with Oscar. I promise I will not leave this seat.'

She shook her head. 'But if he wakes up he's going to expect to see me. He'll want *me.*'

'I know.' Reid nodded. 'And if he wakes, I will get them to get you straight away.'

The indecision on her face was nearly his undoing. She was clearly torn between a mother's need to be with her child and the needs of her fatigued body. He wanted to drag her into his arms, tell her that he loved her and that everything was going to be okay. That he was here for Oscar as well as her.

But it wasn't the right time for that.

'You don't have to do this all by yourself any more, Trinity,' he whispered. 'I'm here for you. *I'm here.* Let me do this. Please?'

A tear rolled down her face. 'You'll get them to fetch me if he wakes?'

Reid slid a palm onto her cheek, smearing the tear in its track, his heart bursting with love. *This was big.* She was trusting him with Oscar. 'I promise.'

Then he leaned in and kissed her again. As he had this morning. As he hoped he'd be able to do a lot more.

She seemed less startled this time, which was heartening but probably spoke more about her exhaustion than anything else. He stood and stepped back so she could ease out of the chair, sitting in her place as soon as she'd vacated it, sliding his hand over the top of Oscar's as soon as she withdrew hers.

The weight of her trust was a precious gift and he wouldn't let her down.

Trinity couldn't believe how quickly Oscar improved. Five days later he was off all oxygen and they were on a normal hospital ward. He'd hovered on the verge of needing further assistance for two days, but then he'd turned a corner and started to pick up and had recovered so quickly. They were even talking about discharge for him tomorrow.

His respiratory specialist was very happy. And she was over the moon. Being dragged back into the abyss of hospitalisation again had been scary and disheartening, but seeing how much stronger his lungs were now gave Trinity great hope for the future.

Of course he was ultra-clingy now, which was normal for him after being so sick. Trinity didn't mind, nor did she blame him. Not even at ten o'clock when he was squirming restlessly in his sleep on her lap in the small recliner *beside* his bed instead of *in* his roomy hospital bed.

The curtain she'd pulled around their bed space earlier so Oscar wouldn't keep getting distracted by the goings-on flicked back a little. She glanced up to find Reid grinning at her.

'Hey,' he said, voice low.

She smiled back. She couldn't help it. Her heart did a funny little giddy-up. He'd visited twice every day. Once with Eddie and then later at night, just him. 'Hey.'

Strictly speaking, now they were out of HDU, it was after visiting hours but being a doctor—and a hottie—got him certain privileges with the nurses. And Trinity looked forward to his night visits with all the stupidity of a lovesick teenager.

Ever since he'd told her she didn't have to do it by herself any more, she'd been spinning hopeless fantasies about their future.

'Is he asleep?' he asked, navigating between the end of the bed and the curtain until he reached the hard plastic chair beside the recliner.

'Yes.' She glanced at Oscar's face, relaxed in slumber. 'Mostly.'

He chuckled as he pulled the seat around, so it was facing the recliner, his thighs wedged either side of the arm, the denim of his jeans pulling taut across his quads.

'You want me to switch with you so you can go and have a shower?'

The last few nights, Trinity had used Reid's visits to have a shower, entrusting Oscar to Reid's care. 'I actually had a shower earlier this afternoon when Oscar was asleep.'

The look of surprise on Reid's face was comical. 'He *must* be better,' Reid teased.

Trinity took it good-naturedly. 'Yes. Thank goodness.'

It was also good to not be her usual bedraggled mess. Reid always turned up fresh and clean and smelling wonderful whereas she was all rumpled and smelled like hospital food and disinfectant.

But not tonight. She was in jeans and a long-sleeved T-shirt—the least baggy one she owned—and she was wearing one of those fancy spray deodorants that someone had left behind in the parent showers.

She smelled like vanilla and pop rocks.

They chatted about Oscar and their respective days and the weather and Christmas and a bunch of other things.

'There was a message on the answering machine for you,' Reid said, after they'd run out of

their usual topics. 'From a Wendy someone…
wanting you to ring her back.'

Trinity frowned. Wendy?

'Wendy Argos, maybe?' Reid said, his brow
scrunched as he tried to remember the name.

'Oh. Argent.' Trinity nodded. 'She's a real-estate agent. It must be about one of the apartments
I had my name down for.'

With everything else on her plate Trinity hadn't
given a thought to her housing situation all week.
She'd resigned herself to Christmas with Reid
and Eddie a few weeks ago and, if she was honest, she'd been looking forward to it.

It didn't seem to bring Reid any joy either if
his, 'Oh,' was anything to go by.

'It's a good thing,' she told him. And herself.
Because it was.

He opened his mouth to say something but shut
it again and said, 'Yes. Of course.'

But he didn't sound very convinced.

'Well, we can't…stay with you for ever, Reid,'
she said even as the idea fluttered seductively
like a sugar-coated butterfly just out of her reach.

He looked at her for long moments, his gaze
searching and assessing. 'Why not?' he asked
finally, leaning forward on his elbows, his gaze

earnest. He'd kept his voice low but the frustration in it was barely disguised.

Trinity blinked. 'Because…'

Because they came from different worlds. Because he had itchy feet and she needed roots. Because she couldn't live with him and pretend not to love him.

'Don't go,' he said. 'Stay.'

'Reid?' Trinity's heart all but stopped in her chest. It wasn't fair of him to dangle something so seductive in front of her. 'What are you talking about?'

'I'm talking about being in love with you.'

Trinity stared at him. He was *in love* with her? But…? Her pulse quickened. 'You love me?'

'Yes.'

She shook her head, dazed by the admission. He looked serious but she dared not even hope he was telling the truth. 'I…don't understand. Why?'

Why would he love someone like her?

He leaned forward in the chair and grabbed the hand that wasn't wrapped around Oscar. 'Because of your pluck and your gumption and how fiercely you love Oscar. And how you are with Eddie and how much Ginger adores you. And how nice you are to everyone despite how bad things have been for you and… *God*.' He shoved a hand through his hair. 'Because of your mouth.'

Trinity couldn't believe what she was hearing. 'My…mouth?'

'Yes.' He gave a half-laugh and kissed the hand he'd enclosed in both of his. 'I stood here that first night looking down at you when you'd fallen asleep at Oscar's bedside and I just…knew. I'd been telling myself it was just *like* I felt and that I had to forget what we'd done in bed and be your friend, especially *now*, but then I realised you'd been under my skin since that first day. When you rescued Pops. And how you would have started that damn car through pride alone if it had been remotely possible. And it just flooded in and it keeps flooding in and I can't bear the thought of you and Oscar being anywhere else but with me and Pops.'

'Reid…' She searched his face, his gorgeous lumberjack face. He looked one hundred per cent serious. Her heart banged in her chest—slow and loud. Her blood poured thick and slug-gish through her veins. 'I thought you wanted to move on. Not settle down.'

He buried his face in his hands again, kissing

her fingers once, twice, three times. 'I did. And then I fell in love with you and I realise *nothing* else matters.'

Trinity shook her head, too overwhelmed to believe it. 'I…don't know what to say.'

'God, *Trinity*… I love you too would be *really* nice about now.'

Trinity smiled as she let everything go inside her and let her love flood in too. '*Of course* I love you. I realised that night in bed with you. I realised I hadn't just let you into my body but into my heart. I'm pretty sure it would have made me miserable in the weeks to come but I've been kinda—'

She glanced at a stirring Oscar. 'Preoccupied.'

He dropped his forehead to their clasped hands and dragged in some deep breaths. 'Thank God,' he finally said, glancing up at her, a broad grin lighting his whole face.

'So you'll stay. You and Oscar?'

Trinity wanted to cherish the moment. Her son was getting better, Reid loved her and he wanted them to stay. But…she needed to be sure. She needed Reid to be sure. Because she wasn't the only person in this equation.

'Are you sure, Reid? Are you sure this isn't

some misplaced sense of honour or duty or some weird ex-army need to protect me? I love you and nothing would make me happier than to be with you but only if you *love* me.'

He shook his head emphatically. 'This is not about honour or protection, Trinity. I know what that feels like. This is something I've *never* felt before. I *am* in love with you.'

Sincerity shone in his eyes and his voice rang with conviction. She believed him. But still she pressed. 'I have a child. I can't just enter into relationships lightly. My parents did that. *Your* parents did that. And it screws kids up. If you take me on, you gotta take on Oscar.'

'You think I don't know you guys come as a team? You think I don't love Oscar as much as I love you?' His tone was full of reproach. 'Because I do, Trinity. And besides, you take me on you gotta take on Eddie. And that might get really rough.'

Trinity knew how much Reid was already dreading that time.

'We both come with dependants,' he said, kissing her hand again. 'It just...' he shrugged '...makes us a bigger, happier family.'

A bigger, happier family. The one thing Trinity had always craved.

'That sounds wonderful,' she whispered, her vision blurring with tears, her heart singing in her chest.

He leaned forward then, careful not to disturb Oscar as he kissed the tears from her cheek then pressed his lips to hers. Trinity sighed against his mouth, lapping up the gentle kiss full of love and compassion and all the years to come.

'Why are you kissing Reid, Mummy?'

Startled, they broke apart to find Oscar staring at them. Trinity, her mind blank, her cheeks heating, groped around for *something* to say. God, how did she explain to a five-year-old what was happening with her and Reid?

And how much was too much information?

'Because she loves me,' Reid said simply, smiling at Oscar then at her.

Trinity blushed some more. 'Yeah.' She smiled. 'Because I love him.'

Oscar reached out and patted Reid's beard. 'I love you too, Reid.'

And Trinity's heart overflowed.

* * * * *

LET'S TALK

Romance

For exclusive extracts, competitions and special offers, find us online:

- **f** facebook.com/millsandboon
- **⊙** @millsandboonuk
- **🐦** @millsandboon

Or get in touch on 0844 844 1351*

For all the latest titles coming soon, visit millsandboon.co.uk/nextmonth

Want even more
ROMANCE?

Join our bookclub today!

'Mills & Boon books, the perfect way to escape for an hour or so.'

Miss W. Dyer

'Excellent service, promptly delivered and very good subscription choices.'

Miss A. Pearson

'You get fantastic special offers and the chance to get books before they hit the shops'

Mrs V. Hall

Visit millsandbook.co.uk/Bookclub and save on brand new books.

MILLS & BOON